Kate was stunned by Van's obvious anger

"What's got into him?" she asked in utter dismay.

"He's jealous," said her uncle, stating the obvious.

"Jealous? Of whom—of what? Because we would have the center of the stage and he'd only be the accompanist?"

"No, of course not." Her uncle spoke indulgently. "He thinks he's in love with you—and maybe he is. He also thinks Carlo has designs upon you. If that's so, it would hardly make for a harmonious trio, one must admit."

"But why didn't he explain?" cried Kate. "If he feels like that, I'll drop Carlo. At least, I mean . . . ." she stopped and suddenly looked extremely startled.

"Well, what exactly do you mean?" inquired Warrender. "The suggestion of a concert tour came from Carlo. In those circumstances he can drop you."

MARY BURCHELL

is also the author of these

Harlequin Romances

1405—THE CURTAIN RISES
1431—THE OTHER LINDING GIRL
1455—GIRL WITH A CHALLENGE
1474—MY SISTER CELIA
1508—CHILD OF MUSIC
1543—BUT NOT FOR ME
1567—DO NOT GO, MY LOVE
1587—MUSIC OF THE HEART
1632—ONE MAN'S HEART
1655—IT'S RUMOURED IN THE VILLAGE
1704—EXCEPT MY LOVE
1733—CALL AND I'LL COME
1767—UNBIDDEN MELODY
1792—PAY ME TOMORROW
1811—STRANGERS MAY MARRY
1834—SONG CYCLE
1871—THE BRAVE IN HEART
1890—TELL ME MY FORTUNE
1919—JUST A NICE GIRL
1936—REMEMBERED SERENADE
1947—THE GIRL IN THE BLUE DRESS
1964—UNDER THE STARS OF PARIS
2043—ELUSIVE HARMONY
2061—HONEY
2290—BARGAIN WIFE
2359—NIGHTINGALES
2379—YOURS WITH LOVE

Masquerade with Music

by

MARY BURCHELL

Harlequin Books

TORONTO • NEW YORK • LOS ANGELES • LONDON
AMSTERDAM • PARIS • SYDNEY • HAMBURG
STOCKHOLM • ATHENS • TOKYO • MILAN

Original hardcover edition published in 1982
by Mills & Boon Limited

ISBN 0-373-02528-9

Harlequin Romance first edition February 1983

CHAPTER ONE

'BUT, Oscar, you can't actually refuse to see the girl!' Anthea Warrender glanced in half amused protest at her husband. 'She is your niece, after all.'

'She is not my niece,' replied the famous conductor without even looking up from his score. 'She is merely the daughter of the designing widow who caught my elder brother.'

'Was she a designing widow?' Anthea enquired curiously.

'She was a widow who took every advantage offered by a long sea voyage. I take it that is what is meant by "designing". Anyway——' Warrender shrugged—'it's all years ago. They settled in New Zealand, so I never met either her or the daughter. Nor indeed my brother after that.'

'Were you quite close to him in the earlier years?'

'Close to him?' Warrender did look up then and considered the question. 'If you mean in a very personal sense—no. We wished each other well, of course, and I admired him for his academic qualities. In fact——' he looked reflective—'I think he probably had the better brain of the two of us.'

'Unprejudiced as I am, I question that,' Anthea smiled.

'True, nevertheless,' he replied with characteristic realism. 'I was more worldly, I suppose, and had my own particular musical gifts. But he was almost a genius in a slightly vague way. I presume that was how she caught him.'

'Well, if she made him happy——' began Anthea. Then, '*Did* she make him happy?'

'I have no idea.' Warrender shrugged again, and Anthea looked down once more at the letter he had tossed into her lap.

'She says the girl has a very beautiful voice and great stage presence,' she observed.

'She wouldn't be the first mother to make that claim for a totally ungifted daughter,' was the cynical reply. 'I see no reason why this one should be an exception to the rule.'

'It's an attractive name, with an odd similarity to yours,' mused Anthea. 'Olga Warrender——'

'The girl has no claim to the attractive name,' cut in her husband shortly. 'She is not a Warrender.'

'Unless your brother chose to adopt her and give her his name. What was the mother's name before her second marriage?'

'How should I know? One of those ordinary names, if I remember rightly. Not quite Smith or Brown. Simpson or something like that. In his rare letters my brother always referred to her as Lucy.'

'She signs herself Lucretia,' observed Anthea.

'She would. That Borgia touch would appeal to her, I imagine. She wrote—probably under that name.'

'Oh, she *wrote*? Then she too had her gifts.' Anthea glanced up with fresh interest.

'Unfortunately, yes. She was what is called, I

believe, a gossip writer,' said Warrender disdain-fully. 'Terrible stuff, very personal and highly-coloured. I wouldn't have known about it except for the fact that she nearly got herself involved in a libel action just before my brother died. I think it cost him quite a packet to get things hushed up.' He paused and then just said. '*Lucretia*, my God!' in a tone of ineffable contempt.

Anthea laughed; that very pretty laugh which was one of her special charms. 'You really are in a bad temper, aren't you, darling?' she said equably.

'I expect so.' Her husband gave her his own rare smile, and then sighed impatiently. 'I miss my in-valuable Miss Caterham more than I could have believed possible. I hardly realised her value for the last ten years, until she became ill. Each secre-tary sent by the agency proves more idiotic than the last.'

'I know, I know,' Anthea said sympathetically. 'I always said Isobel Caterham was a pearl beyond price. But we'll find someone presently. Meanwhile, I'm just off to the nursing home to see her. Shall I give her your love?'

'No, that would be excessive,' Warrender replied with great exactness. 'Give her my good wishes and all the fruit and flowers and anything else she would fancy. And tell her I miss her,' he added suddenly, for he was on the whole a just man.

'I will,' Anthea promised. Then she slipped the discussed letter into her handbag, kissed her hus-band and departed to visit his invaluable secretary at the very expensive nursing home to which he had insisted on sending her.

For her part, Isobel Caterham had not reached the age of forty-eight without realising that she was indeed a treasure. She would have been a fool if she had failed to do so; and no fool would have remained Oscar Warrender's secretary for long. She thought the sun, moon and morning star shone out of her employer and his wife, and if countless operatic enthusiasts thought the same, how could she be wrong?

'You mustn't worry so much about him,' Anthea told her kindly. 'He's managing quite well, although he said I was to tell you that he misses you.'

'It's nice to be missed, but——' Isobel Caterham sighed—'he *can't* be managing very well. He hates changes in his immediate personnel. Who has he at present, Lady Warrender?'

'We-ell,' Anthea had to admit, 'we're between two possibilities, you might say.'

'You mean,' retorted her husband's secretary shrewdly, 'that he's just dispensed with someone impossible and is now waiting without much hope for the next one.'

Anthea gave a vexed little laugh and agreed that this was more or less the case. 'But,' she added, 'the new one comes with the highest recommendations from an agency specialising in international staff. Dermot Deane employed her recently when he was in Paris and says she's excellent.'

'Mr Deane is a gifted impresario,' conceded Miss Caterham rather stiffly, 'but I wouldn't regard him as the best judge of a secretary likely to suit Sir Oscar. In Paris, you say?' she slightly pursed her lips. 'Do you mean she's French?'

'Oh, no. Canadian, I think. At least, Dermot said she came by way of Canada to France. And now, providentially it seems, she has ended up in London. Anyway, my dear, let's hope for the best, while admitting that you yourself are quite irreplaceable.' Anthea smiled at her with real affection. 'Even Oscar must put up with a few inconveniences occasionally. All we want is for you to get well.'

'Just so long as he isn't irritated to a degree that interferes with his ART,' said Miss Caterham in capital letters.

'Quite so,' agreed Anthea, nobly stifling a yawn. For, though she adored her husband, she sometimes found the adulation surrounding the famous conductor rather trying. It never failed to astonish her that he himself seemed unaware of it, or at least totally indifferent to it. Resisting the desire to say that it might not hurt him to have to make the best of things for once, she rose and prepared to take her leave.

'Oh, Lady Warrender,' cried Miss Caterham just as she reached the door, 'you won't forget that he *must* make time to see that interesting man who's doing a book on contemporary conductors, will you? It's unthinkable that an authoritative book on famous conductors should not include Sir Oscar.'

'I'll remember,' Anthea promised. 'What was his name, did you say?'

'Evander Merton.'

'Oh, dear!' said Anthea and finally departed.

As she re-entered the apartment in St James's,

for some reason, Anthea clearly recalled the first time she had come there—a nervous, aspiring young singer from the provinces, terrified by the fact that she was to sing for the famous Oscar Warrender for the first time. Then she realised that it was the sound of a charming speaking voice, with a hint of suppressed nervousness in it, which had twanged that chord of memory. She heard her husband ask an abrupt question and then the musical, faintly nervous voice replied.

'The new secretary,' she decided and, mildly curious after what Dermot Deane had said about her, she went into the studio.

Her husband was sitting at his desk and facing him sat a quietly dressed young woman, listening to what he was saying with an air of genuine interest and attention. She was in the full light from the window, so that the afternoon sunshine added a touch of pure gold to her smooth fair hair.

She rose to her feet immediately as Anthea came in and Oscar Warrender said, 'This is my wife, Miss Grayson,' and then to Anthea, 'Miss Grayson is going to replace Miss Caterham for the time being.'

'I thought we were still discussing no more than possibilities, Sir Oscar,' said the girl, and as she smiled Anthea noticed a gleam of something like mischief in her quite remarkable grey eyes.

'No,' said Warrender. 'I made my decision ten minutes ago. When can you start?'

'Tomorrow morning. Unless you have a backlog of work which requires attention this evening.'

Warrender gave a short, not displeased laugh.

But before he could say anything the telephone rang beside him.

He picked up the receiver and said, 'Yes?' in a non-committal tone. 'Who? Evander Merton? Wait a moment. I'll ask my secretary.' Then, seeing that Anthea was making signs, he put his hand over the mouthpiece and asked, 'Have you ever heard of him?'

'Yes, of course,' Anthea explained rapidly. 'He's the man who's writing that book about conductors. Isobel says it's important and that you must be in the book. At least *see* him, Oscar,' she added as her husband made a face.

'You deal with this,' Warrender said, and calmly handed the telephone to the young woman on the other side of the desk.

Putting her hand over the mouthpiece in her turn, she simply asked, ' "Yes" or "no"?'

'Yes,' replied Warrender. 'But don't be fulsome and don't commit me to anything.'

'Mr Merton, this is Sir Oscar's secretary speaking,' she said in that pleasant voice. 'It's about the book you're writing, isn't it? Sir Oscar is very much occupied at the present time. But would it be a good idea if you had a word with me first, and then perhaps we could arrange for him to see you personally and discuss things further? It would? Just a minute while I look at the diary.'

Warrender pushed towards her across the desk a slip of paper on which he had written in his bold, legible handwriting. 'Tomorrow afternoon. Three o'clock. Here.'

'Would tomorrow afternoon at three suit you,

Mr Merton? It would? Then here, at Killigrew Mansions. The hall porter will bring you up.—Not at all. Thank you. Goodbye.'

She replaced the receiver, Anthea laughed outright, and Warrender smiled grimly as he said, 'You're engaged, in case I had not made that clear already. Can you be here tomorrow morning at nine-thirty?'

'Certainly,' the girl said, and then she took courteous leave of her future employer and his wife.

'She seems reasonably efficient,' commented Warrender, as they heard the front door close.

'She has remarkably beautiful eyes,' replied Anthea.

'I didn't notice,' said her husband.

'Don't be affected, darling. Of course you did,' Anthea told him. 'With almost every artist you've ever handled——'

'She is not an artist,' Warrender interrupted. 'Not even an aspiring one, I trust.' But then he added, 'Yes, her eyes are remarkable. I have an idea they don't miss much, for one thing. She wasn't flustered over having to play my secretary without warning. Though I noticed her hand shook slightly as she took the phone.'

'You see?' Anthea laughed triumphantly. 'You did notice most things about her. I expect she was nervous, poor girl,' she added compassionately. 'But she hid it well. Anyway, she'll have to be cool and collected to stay the course with you. What's her name, by the way?'

'I told you when I introduced her—Grayson.'

'No, her other name.'

Warrender consulted the agency form and said, 'It's given here as Kate. Katherine or Kathleen, I suppose. Modishly shortened in the silly manner of today.—So long as she doesn't attempt to call me Oscar,' he added, as he drew his score towards him once more.

Kate Grayson, as she left Killigrew Mansions and started to walk across the Park, would have been surprised to know that the Warrenders were assessing her as a cool and collected young woman. In point of fact she had never felt less cool or collected in her life. On the contrary, her admirably shaped legs felt strangely weak and insecure, and it was only with a deliberate effort that she unclenched her hands as she walked along. Presently she came to a shaded bench, where she sat down and allowed herself to relax. Then, as she realised that she was completely alone, she permitted herself the indulgence of saying aloud, but softly, 'Well— I'm in!'

After a while she opened her large handbag and drew out a writing pad and deliberately wrote,

'Dear Mother, My Uncle Oscar is all that people say—curt, authoritative, quite unfairly handsome—and married to the prettiest and most friendly person I've met in years.

'No, I'm not a protégée yet. Not even a humble student. And I rather doubt if I shall ever be either, so don't start building castles in the air. I met his impresario in Paris, where I managed to do some secretarial work for him. That gave me the edge on anyone else applying to be Uncle Oscar's temporary secretary—so, you see, I was right to insist on a top secretarial training. I'll let you know when I have a place of my own. At present I'm in a modest hotel. And I'm using a variation on my own name, of course. I'm being exceedingly discreet, as you see—and I IMPLORE YOU TO BE THE SAME. You did promise that I should handle this my own way, remember. All my love, Kate.'

The next morning she presented herself at the Warrenders' apartment in good time, and was admitted by a maid who took her to a small but pleasant office. Here, thanks to the methods of the invaluable Isobel Caterham, she had little difficulty in finding the well-arranged office supplies; and a quick examination of the filing cabinet showed her that all was in excellent order up to three weeks ago, after which some odd muddles seemed to have taken place. She rapidly brought order out of recent chaos and then fell to studying the pile of correspondence in the 'In' tray.

On some of the letters Warrender had scribbled a trenchant comment or two, on the rest merely 'Yes' or 'No'. She was just familiarising herself with the way Miss Caterham had conducted previous correspondence with some of these people when Warrender came in, greeted her quite pleasantly and asked merely. 'Is all that clear?'

Resisting the craven temptation to say, 'Yes,' and chance her luck in guessing what was really required, she said calmly,

'No. Some of them are quite straightforward, of course. But when, for instance——' she reached for one letter—'you say, "The man's an ass," do you wish me to convey that information to him bluntly or tactfully? or were you perhaps just letting off steam?'

For the first time she saw Oscar Warrender laugh heartily. Then he came to stand beside her as he took the letter from her, and she was keenly and rather frighteningly aware of his height and his overwhelming presence.

'I was just letting off steam,' he said, and she found his unexpected frankness oddly engaging. 'Let him know that I can't agree with him, but you needn't be harsh. He's an old man and, now I come to think of it, he was once very good to me when I was young and brash.'

'Were you ever brash?' she asked with interest.

'Oh, yes. Most young people are either brash or boring,' he told her goodhumouredly. 'And I was never boring,' he added with no false modesty. 'Do what you can with the rest of those. I have to go to rehearsal now. Later you can ask me about anything you find impossible to tackle.'

'And Mr Merton? Who's coming here this afternoon, you remember. Do you really want me to interview him on your behalf? and, if so, am I to hold out any hope that you'll see him yourself later?'

'Use your own judgment about him,' said Warrender. 'I can't imagine I would really want him to "write me up" as the horrible phrase is. That sort of thing makes me cringe.' She thought she had never seen anyone less likely to cringe than Oscar Warrender. But then he went on, 'I have an impossible sister-in-law—on the other side of the world, fortunately—who writes on those lines.

She's trying to force her ghastly child on me at the moment. But we'll deal with that later.'

Then he went off, leaving Kate Grayson to stare at the door he had just closed behind him and murmur thoughtfully, 'Yes, we'll deal with that later.'

She worked steadily during the rest of the morning. Anthea Warrender looked in once, to ask how she was getting on, and to supply a useful comment on one or two of the letters. Then she explained that she herself was going out to lunch but that Kate would have lunch served to her in the apartment unless she chose to make other arrangements.

'In any case, you'll want some sort of break before your afternoon stint,' she said. 'It's a glorious day and we're quite near the Park, as you know. Don't drive yourself too hard. You seem to have got through a lot of work.' She glanced respectfully at the pile of answered correspondence. 'Is my husband leaving you to tackle Mr Evander Merton on his behalf?'

'Yes,' Kate smiled.

'He sounds rather academic and elderly, doesn't he?' Anthea said curiously.

'Unless his friends call him "Van". In which case he may be tough and exuberant,' Kate suggested.

'Did he *sound* like that?' Anthea asked with interest.

'I believe he did, now I come to think of it.'

'Well, he'll need to be tough if he's going to persuade Oscar to let him write about him. My husband is rather prejudiced about that sort of thing.

Unfortunately, he has a sister-in-law who——'

'Yes, so he told me,' interrupted Kate, suddenly unable to bear to hear any more strictures on that subject.

'Did he really?' Anthea looked amused. Then, oddly enouth, she used exactly the same words as her husband. 'Well, use your own judgment about the man.' Though characteristically she added, 'It would hardly be fair to be prejudiced beforehand just because Oscar has a sister-in-law he doesn't like.'

Left to herself, Kate finished dealing with anything she felt able to tackle on her own initiative. Then, reluctantly leaving what promised to be a very interesting report on some unknown opera, she had her excellent lunch and went out for a breath of fresh air before returning to the apartment with some curiosity about her expected visitor.

He arrived with admirable punctuality just as Big Ben boomed out three o'clock across the Park; and when the Warrenders' maid admitted him to the office Kate immediately registered the fact that he was neither academic nor elderly in appearance.

Nor was he the exuberant type, she thought, though tough he might be. Certainly the glance of his curiously brilliant blue eyes was very direct, his handshake was firm to the point of hard, and though he smiled pleasantly, she noticed that the line of his jaw was very determined. Mr Evander Merton knew where he was going, she decided in that first minute, and he expected the world to stand aside for him, as the old Italian proverb has it.

'It was kind of you to see me at such short notice,' he said formally, as he took the chair she indicated.

'Not at all.' She was equally polite and formal. 'Sir Oscar thought a preliminary discussion might be useful. Would you like to put me in the picture? I came to England only recently, so if I say I don't really know anything about your book you mustn't take that as a slight.'

'I don't.' His quick smile was more friendly. 'I'm not the touchy type of author who requires kid-glove treatment. There's no special reason why you should have heard of my book, particularly if you don't live in London. Does this mean that you've only been with Sir Oscar a short time?'

'It's my first day,' she told him, and then wondered what it was about him that had made her so frank.

'You don't say!' He looked at her now with a sort of amused speculation. 'And he left you to interview me on your own?'

'Oh, dear! Does that sound like another slight?'

'No, it sounds as though you made a powerful impression on a reputedly difficult man.'

She laughed. 'Well, shall we start at the beginning? This book deals with several conductors, I understand?'

'Four, counting Sir Oscar, if I can persuade him to let me include him. The other three have already consented, and a good deal of work has been done on them.'

'Who are the other three? I think Sir Oscar would want to know in whose company he would be finding himself.'

'Of course.' He named the other three, and Kate recognised them all as something like world-famous and certainly highly regarded in musical circles. 'My own qualifications,' he went on, 'include the fact that I have a musical degree, one of my subjects being conducting, although no one is going to put me among the world's top ten. But at least I know what I'm talking about technically. In fact I did a modest amount of conducting and coaching in New Zealand the year before last.'

'In New Zealand?' She tried to keep that slightly wary note out of her voice, but it seemed she had not succeeded, because he glanced at her curiously and asked, 'Do you know New Zealand?'

'I've been there. But do go on. You don't mind if I make a few notes, do you? It will help when I report to Sir Oscar.'

'Of course not.' He continued then to give her a brief but comprehensive account of the way he intended to deal with his subject, and Kate realised that there was something very practical and professional about his approach. So much so that she interrupted him to say,

'You must surely have had some writing experience?'

'Oh, certainly! Didn't I mention that? I've done a good bit of musical journalism in the course of knocking about the world. My publishers would hardly have taken me seriously otherwise. They're Crane & Abercrombie, by the way.'

'Have they actually commissioned the book?' She was a good deal impressed, but managed to conceal the fact.

'Yes, but with one proviso.' He hesitated, then added, 'I'd better put my cards on the table and admit that they insist that Sir Oscar is one of the four dealt with.'

'I see.' She bit her lip thoughtfully, and after a moment he asked impulsively, 'From your admittedly limited knowledge of him, would you say he would be difficult to persuade?'

'I think no one would persuade him to do something to which he was strongly opposed,' she replied candidly. 'But with regard to the book, I gathered the impression that although he wasn't enthusiastic, nor was he dismissing it out of hand.'

'Well, come, that's something. And do you propose to speak for me or against me?' he asked, and he looked directly at her.

Her first instinct was to make a friendly reply, but that oddly chilling reference to New Zealand suddenly recurred to her, and she found she could say no more than a stiff, 'I shall try to be factual and fair in my report, of course.'

'That sounds like my exit line.' He made a slight face, but as he rose to go he held out his hand to her and perforce she had to accept it. Then, without releasing her hand, he went on, 'Please tell him that although there'll naturally have to be a certain amount of personal detail and history, I'm most concerned with the artistic side of his life. I think I know one reason why he's prejudiced against——'

Kate suddenly snatched her hand away and

he looked surprised.

'I—I thought I heard the other phone,' she murmured. 'No—it's all right. You were saying——?'

'Nothing very important. But I happen to know there was a rather menacing writer in his own family who specialised in digging up irrelevant chit-chat. It caused some trouble, and he may think all personality writers are the same. I'd be grateful if you would assure him I'm not like that at all.'

'I will,' said Kate coldly. Then, in an effort to appear at least reasonably friendly, she accompanied him to the front door. She was therefore standing at the open door of the apartment when the lift slid smoothly upward and out stepped quite the most attractive-looking man she had ever seen.

He and Mr Merton exchanged nods, her first visitor departed in the lift and the newcomer said, as though he had every right to enquire, 'Who was that? a singer?'

'No. A writer,' replied Kate. 'Can I do anything for you?'

'Indeed you can.' She noticed then that there was a slight foreign intonation in the voice, and she thought there was what she described to herself as 'something Latin' in the way he smiled at her. 'You can stop guarding that door as though you thought I might have come to steal the silver. Sir Oscar is expecting me, but I'm ten minutes early for my appointment.'

She stood aside then, but she felt bound to ask, 'Who are you, though?'

'You don't *know*?' He was so engagingly astonished that the question was curiously devoid of conceit. 'I'm Carlo Ertlinger, and please don't say you've never heard of me.'

'I know the name, of course,' she conceded smilingly.

'But you've never heard me sing?' And when she shook her head he exclaimed, 'Where *have* you been? You'd better come and hear me on Friday night. I'm singing Don Giovanni.'

Kate nearly said, 'How appropriate,' but stopped herself in time, which gave him the chance to say,

'Warrender is conducting and Anthea is singing Elvira. It will be good, even though Warrender insists that I need some final words of advice this afternoon. I'll see you have tickets,' he added carelessly, 'if you'll give me your name.'

'My name is Kate Grayson.' They were in the studio by now. 'And I'd simply love to come, if you're serious, but——'

'Of course I'm serious. Can't you see how solemn I am?' he said, as his laughing eyes challenged her. 'There'll be two tickets, Kate, at the box office in your name——'

'One will be sufficient,' she assured him, wishing she felt a little less dazed by the speed of events.

'Impossible! Don't tell me that with that hair and that smile you go to the opera unaccompanied.'

'I don't know anyone in London yet,' she began.

'No one to take you out to supper afterwards, you mean?' And then, as she slowly shook her head, he took her hand, kissed it lightly and said, 'Then you shall come to supper with me, Kate.

Come round to my dressing-room after the performance and we'll arrange to go somewhere nice.'

Then, before she could either accept, which seemed crazy—or refuse, which seemed impossible—she heard someone put a key in the front door and a moment later her employer entered.

'Hello, Carlo.' He spoke quite genially, but added drily, 'Stop flirting with my new secretary.'

'How do you know I was flirting?' replied the young man with an injured air.

'By the same token as I know what a kitten does when it sees a saucer of cream.' replied Warrender. 'Now let's see what can be done with that scene you muffed at rehearsal.' And he dismissed Kate to the office with a brief nod.

She went back to her desk and tried, not very successfully, to concentrate on her work. She was almost immediately distracted by the sound of a piano being played and then this was joined by a rich, vibrant voice singing what she recognised as a passage from Mozart's *Don Giovanni* which she happened to know well.

She stopped what she was doing, having decided that it would be sacrilege to go on typing while those beautiful sounds were seeping through the wall. But apparently not everything was going smoothly. There was a certain amount of repetition and once she heard Warrender's voice raised. Then suddenly the piano playing stopped, the door of the studio was flung open and a moment later her employer came into the office and said,

'You don't by any chance sing, do you, Miss Grayson?'

'*Sing?*' She looked as startled as she felt. 'Yes—I mean no!'

'Well, which do you mean?' he asked disagreeably.

She swallowed, tried to decide whether this were the chance of a lifetime or merely the trap which had been waiting for her ever since she left home.

'I mean that I'm probably not what you would regard as a serious singer——'

'Probably not,' he agreed dryly. 'That would be too much to ask of heaven at a moment's notice. Can you read music and keep in tune?'

She swallowed again. 'Yes, I—I think I could do that.'

He made a peremptory summoning gesture with his head and she followed him into the studio, where Carlo Ertlinger was leaning against the piano looking amused.

'Don't tell me she actually knows the role of Zerlina,' he said.

'No,' replied Warrender, 'but——'

'I do, as a matter of fact,' said Kate timidly. 'I—I once belonged to an amateur operatic society.'

'God help us,' said Warrender, and handed her a vocal score.

As he gave her a few remarkably lucid instructions, she decided rapidly that this was not the moment to show off the most that she could do. Too many explanations and questions would follow if she betrayed anything like a professional standard of performance. All that was required of her was that she should act as foil to Carlo Ertlinger while Warrender took him through a particularly tricky passage or two.

She cleared her throat, managed to look even more timid and lost than she really felt, and sang softly and tentatively when required. But nothing could hide the fact that she was extremely musical, and she could not bring herself to make a deliberate mistake.

At the end of a nerve-racking quarter of an hour, Oscar Warrender pronounced himself relatively satisfied.

'*That's* the way you do it on Friday,' he told Ertlinger sternly. And then, to Kate, 'Thank you, Miss Grayson. You're very musical and that's quite a pretty voice you have, though I doubt if you're using your full potential.'

Then she was free to go, her knees shaking and a strained smile on her face.

Presently she heard the volatile baritone depart and almost immediately Warrender came into the office and asked, though without much interest, 'What's this about your going to supper with Carlo after the performance on Friday?'

'I'm not quite sure,' Kate confessed. 'He seemed incredulous that I'd never heard him and was kind enough to offer me two tickets. Then when I explained I wouldn't need more than one as I should be alone he—he added the invitation to supper.'

'I see. Do you want to go?'

'I—suppose most girls would, wouldn't they?'

'I couldn't say. I don't profess to know how "most girls" tick. But you understand that as my secretary you indulge in no gossiping if you go socialising with any of my singers.'

'Of *course* I understand that!' She spoke indignantly, but he seemed unimpressed, for as he went across to his desk to look through one or two papers, he went on, 'And don't praise him too highly after the performance, whatever you may think. He would probably jump to the conclusion that you were quoting me.'

'I'll remember,' she promised a little stiffly. And then, with irresistible curiosity, '*Is* he a good Giovanni, in fact?'

'Not yet. He may be one day if he works hard enough. At the moment he's relying on his natural gifts, a certain amount of charm and good looks, and a great deal of animal magnetism.'

Kate was silent, digesting what she recognised as a very shrewd assessment. Then, without looking up, her employer asked suddenly, 'Where did you learn to sing, Miss Grayson?'

'Where——?' Her heart gave a most uncomfortable lurch. Then, a trifle too carelessly, she said, 'Oh, I had some lessons in my last year or two at school. Our singing teacher——'

Then she stopped dead because her employer was now leaning back in his chair, regarding her with a sort of amused attention.

'Try again,' he said quite pleasantly. 'I'm too old a bird to be put off with tales of some anonymous schoolteacher.'

'Oh——!' She was so discomfited that she flushed almost to the point of tears. Then desperately she said, 'It makes me nervous even to speak about my minor gift with anyone as distinguished as you, Sir Oscar. I'm mortified just to think of my silly contribution this afternoon.'

'You have no reason to be mortified,' he told her. 'It was not at all a bad effort for someone dropped on at a moment's notice while typing—whatever it was you were typing. But I've no wish to embarrass someone who plays down her gifts rather than exaggerating them. I assure you it's quite a novelty for me.—How did you get on with Mr Merton and his book, by the way?'

'Oh——' she had almost forgotten the interview in the agitation of the last hour. 'He spoke very practically and professionally, I thought. The publishers would be Crane & Abercrombie. They've actually commissioned the book, but more or less on the understanding that you're included.'

'Who are the others?'

She told him, and he made a disparaging sound at the mention of the second one, which prompted her to ask curiously, 'You don't regard him as a fine conductor?'

'No. He has a good stick technique, but is a bit of a charlatan. However, he has a big television following and would no doubt help to sell the book,' Warrender conceded realistically.

'Not as much as you would,' she retorted quickly, and then was rather surprised at her own immediate partisanship. For his part he seemed amused and asked her goodhumouredly how often she had heard him conduct.

'Never,' she had to confess. 'Except on records, of course.'

'Well then, I shall have to be on my mettle on Friday,' he said gravely. 'Give me those letters and

I'll sign them now.'

She brought him all the letters she had typed and though he made few comments, he signed them all and she had the idea that he was satisfied.

'Shall I make a personal appointment with Mr Merton for you?' she asked before clearing her desk for the day.

'No, no, let him do the wooing. It would be a mistake to sound eager.' Then as the telephone rang, he added, 'That's probably him now.'

'Already?' Kate looked sceptical.

'He'll think you've gone home by now and that this is his opportunity for a persuasive word or two with me in private,' Warrender asserted. 'Give me the phone.'

She handed it over, and when she heard him say, 'This is Oscar Warrender speaking, Mr Merton,' she had difficulty in stifling a slight laugh. But she felt a tremor of anxiety too, for she wondered why her afternoon visitor was so determined to dispense with her now as an intermediary.

'No, I wouldn't put it that way,' she heard her employer say. 'It's her business to exercise a certain amount of caution before committing me to anything, you know. In point of fact, she gave quite a favourable account of your visit. I think it's time you and I met.'

He held out his hand and Kate immediately put the desk diary into it.

'Let me see—what about Friday morning?— What's that?—Yes. I'm conducting in the evening, but I'm quite capable of holding a sensible conversation in the morning. Shall we say eleven o'clock?—Yes, certainly my secretary will be there. Not to hold a watching brief, merely to make any notes I require.'

He rang off and looked at Kate with some interest.

'What did you do to make him think you had distinct reservations against him and his book?'

'Nothing!' Kate said indignantly. 'I was perfectly polite and——'

'Nothing is more offputting than perfect politeness,' observer her employer. 'No, no, don't start apologising. You did very well. As I told you, it's not necessary to appear too eager at this point. And now it's time you went home.'

Kate resisted the temptation to justify herself further, said goodnight to Sir Oscar and took her departure, feeling suddenly that this was the longest, hardest, most emotionally exhausting day she had ever spent. She had successfully taken up the reins from the incredibly efficient Miss Caterham; she had interviewed—and slightly antagonised—someone who had an unwelcome link with the background she wished to conceal; and she had sung for Oscar Warrender, although hardly in circumstances she would herself have chosen.

In addition, she reminded herself as she made her way home, she had more or less promised to go out to supper with one of the current darlings of the operatic world.

The next day proved very much less exacting. She even snatched time during her lunch hour to go and look at the outside of Covent Garden Opera House for the first time in her life. And as she walked slowly past the entrance and round the corner into Floral Street, her early ambitions stirred within her afresh, and she asked herself, half mockingly, half wistfully, if she really supposed she would ever enter that august building as anything but a member of the audience.

She even peeped inside the stage door, but then retraced her steps almost immediately, with the ridiculously guilty feeling that it was presumptuous of her so much as to glance backstage when she had no claim to be there. She quickened her steps and, as she turned once more into Bow Street, she almost ran into Carlo Ertlinger.

'Kate! How charming.' He caught both her hands in his as though they were very old friends indeed. 'What are you doing here?'

'Gazing in starstruck wonder,' she told him with a laugh. 'It's the first time I've ever seen Covent Garden.'

'The first time?' He sounded incredulous again, and again he said, 'Where *have* you been?'

'Not in London,' she told him. But before he could ask anything further she added quickly, 'But tell me where *you've* been and where you come from. Your name sounds such an odd mixture of Italian and German.'

'It is. My father was Austrian and my mother Italian. It was she who insisted on the "Carlo". And you can call me by it.'

'Thank you. I'll think about it.' Kate smiled because it was difficult not to smile when he looked so boyishly friendly. 'But I must go now or I'll be late.'

'Is Warrender a tyrant to you as well as to us?' he enquired sympathetically.

'Not at all. At least——' she crossed her fingers and laughed—'not so far. But there are such things as office hours, and one expects to keep to them.'

'Charming, conscientious Kate!' Carlo also laughed and bade her goodbye. Then, as she turned away, she found to her surprise that Evander Merton was standing there, apparently waiting to speak to her.

He glanced after the baritone and said, 'We three seem to make a habit of meeting. But I suppose this is a very natural spot for us to run into each other.'

She did not answer that. Instead, on a not very wise impulse, she asked, 'Why did you tell Sir Oscar I was unfriendly when I interviewed you yesterday?'

'Unfriendly?' For the first time she saw him flush and look put out. 'I didn't say *"unfriendly"*. Only that you seemed rather hostile to me and my book.'

'You had no reason to say any such thing,' she retorted, and hailed a passing taxi, with an air of putting an immediate end to a conversation which had hardly begun.

'If I was wrong, I apologise.' He determinedly kept pace with her as she took a few steps towards the taxi. 'I was perhaps over-anxious that he shouldn't be in any way put off.'

'He was not in any way put off—by *me*,' she

replied curtly. And she got into the taxi and drove away without any form of goodbye.

Almost immediately she regretted both her words and her tone of voice. The last thing she wanted was to make an enemy of this man. If he were indeed allowed to undertake this book—and she realised now that instinctively she had been against his doing so—then it would be his business to enquire into the background of Oscar Warrender's life and career. That would not necessarily include many early family details—but he knew about New Zealand and that wretched near-libel action. Just details, of course—but someone less than friendly might concern himself over-much with unwanted details.

'I'll be nice to him when he comes tomorrow,' she told herself. But she wished she had handled him quite differently.

She was still wishing it when he arrived the next morning and was shown into the studio where Oscar Warrender had elected to receive him. Kate herself was seated at the side of his big desk, with no specific duty until her employer should ask her to make a note of anything. She gave their visitor a placatory smile and even managed to whisper, 'Sorry about yesterday. I was in a temper,' as he passed her. But either he did not hear her or chose to ignore her.

Both men were extremely businesslike when it came to the point, and she judged that they were almost immediately en rapport with each other.

'He's good at it,' she thought reluctantly. 'He's done his homework well and knows how to handle

Sir Oscar, with emphasis on his work rather than personal details.' And she began to relax a little herself.

Then Evander Merton said, 'I've done quite a lot of research on your personal background, and collected a useful selection of photographs. It will be for you to make a choice from them, of course.'

'Photographs? Have you got them there?' Warrender looked amused and then interested as his visitor abstracted a file from his case and handed it over.

'Hm—my father!' Warrender laughed as though reminded of something or someone he had almost forgotten. Then he handed the first photograph to Kate, who only just stopped herself from saying, 'Yes, I know that one of him.' For it had hung in the sitting-room at home for many years.

Instead she said, 'He looks rather intimidating.'

'He was. The only man I was ever afraid of, I think,' replied her employer frankly. Then the telephone rang and he picked up the receiver.

'Oh, Dermot! I wondered when you were going to let me hear about that.—Excuse me——' to Evander Merton. Then he dropped into French and turned aside to concentrate on what his impresario was saying. At the same time his visitor got up and strolled across to the window and looked out, politely dissociating himself from the private conversation.

Kate just sat and stared at that pile of photographs which was comfortably within her reach. Then, as though moved by casual curiosity, she drew them towards her and stirred the pile idly with her slightly trembling finger.

Yes, it was there! She had known, with a sort of superstitious instinct, that it would be. The photograph of her mother, her stepfather and herself at fifteen.

Recognisable?—Surely so, even with her hair long and tied back with a big bow of ribbon. To her it seemed impossible that anyone would miss the likeness—with the original herself sitting there, though five years older. It was something she simply could not risk.

Sir Oscar was laughing and completely taken up with his telephone conversation. Evander Merton still stood at the window looking out.

With the lightest of movements Kate slid the photograph from the pile and then on to the floor, at the same time dropping her pencil. Then she stooped to pick them both up. The pencil she restored to the desk in front of her. The photograph now reposed in her handbag beside her chair.

CHAPTER TWO

'I'M sorry, I didn't expect that call to take so long.' Oscar Warrender replaced the receiver and, with an apologetic gesture, indicated that his visitor should return to his seat. 'Let me see—where were we?'

'We were discussing photographs for the book,' replied Evander Merton as he came back from the window. 'Or rather, you were looking through them to make a selection.'

'Yes, of course.' The conductor moved the papers and photographs on his desk and then looked up as the door opened and Anthea came into the room. 'Oh, this is my wife, Mr Merton——' He made the introductions and then said with a smile, 'Have a look at these photographs, Anthea. Most of them taken long before you knew me, I imagine. That's my father.' He handed her the first one. 'I don't think you ever saw a photograph of him, did you?'

'He looks rather intimidating,' Anthea said, using the same word as Kate.

'Sir Oscar says he's the only man he was ever afraid of,' Kate interjected, and managed a convincingly amused little laugh.

'Really?' Anthea glanced curiously at her husband. 'He's very like you, did you know?'

'Yes, of course. That's probably why we didn't

get on.' Warrender picked up another photograph, laughed and said, 'My brother and me at school. I think we'll suppress that. It wouldn't do much for my directorial authority among my singers.'

'It's nice. I like it.' Anthea examined it with attention. 'There's not much likeness, though. At least, not at that age. Have you got one of your brother grown up?'

'I don't see one,' Warrender began. But his visitor leaned forward and started to shuffle through the pile.

'There's quite an attractive one here somewhere,' he said. 'With his wife and stepdaughter.'

'With Lucretia? Oh, do find it,' Anthea exclaimed. 'I'd like to see what she's like—and the daughter too. We're expecting her here some time soon, as a matter of fact. The daughter, I mean.'

'We are not,' her husband corrected her. 'At least, not in this household.'

'You can't show her the door,' Anthea asserted obstinately, while their visitor went through the pile of photographs for the second time, and Kate pinned a stiff smile to her face and tried to look totally unselfconscious. 'She'll probably phone first,' Anthea went on, 'and then what will you do? Or rather, what shall *I* do, if I take the call?'

'Tell her we're leaving for Brazil at dawn,' replied Warrender. 'Have you found the photograph, Mr Merton?'

'No. But I know it's here somewhere.' Looking puzzled, he went through the photographs for the third time, and then shook the file which had contained them.

'It must have dropped on the floor,' suggested Anthea, and obligingly began to look for it. Kate, with a helpful air, joined in the search, secretly wondering how it was that the others apparently remained unaware of the thunderous beating of her heart.

'It's not here!' The vexed astonishment in Evander Merton's voice made Kate clench her teeth to keep them from chattering. Then suddenly she found the cool courage to say, 'You must have left it at home.'

'I did nothing of the kind!' He looked at her almost with open dislike. 'I most carefully checked everything I brought.'

'It doesn't matter,' said Warrender, with an air of such casual dismissal that Kate could have embraced him. 'You'll find it somewhere. Anyway, it isn't a photograph we should use.'

'But I'd have liked to see it,' Anthea objected. 'I want to know what the expected niece looks like.'

There was a moment's pause, during which Kate was suddenly aware that Evander Merton was regarding her with extraordinary attention. Then the terrifying thing he said was, 'Perhaps you will find that out, Lady Warrender, without the assistance of any photograph.'

'Well, yes, I expect so,' Anthea agreed easily. 'She's bound to turn up some time soon and, whatever my husband likes to say, she has some claim on our hospitality.'

This time Warrender refrained from disputing the fact, and contented himself with saying resignedly, 'If only she didn't claim to sing!'

'Does she do that?' Suddenly their visitor sounded amused and, without being able to look up, Kate was aware that he had not taken his eyes from her.

'They nearly all do,' Warrender replied. 'But we're getting away from essentials.' Then he and Evander Merton returned to serious discussion, Kate somehow managed to keep her hand steady as she made any required notes, and Anthea, after some minutes, said she must go as she had an appointment.

Just as she was about to take friendly leave of their visitor she suddenly asked, 'Tell me, does anyone ever call you by your unusual first name?'

'No.' He smiled. 'My friends call me Van.'

'Miss Grayson said they would,' commented Anthea, at which Mr Merton shot a less than friendly look at Miss Grayson, and Anthea took her departure.

It was over at last, the fearful necessity of sitting there under those curious and searching glances which he cast at her from time to time.

'He knows,' she told herself, but then, 'he *can't* know—I'm imagining things.' She tried to command herself to appear quite unselfconscious, to raise her head and look him casually in the face. But for a thousand pounds she could not have done so. All she could do was sit there with her head bent over her notes, and if he thought she was sulking that was the very most she could hope.

Sir Oscar accompanied his visitor to the door, and when he came back into the room he remarked, 'I don't wonder Merton thought you disliked him. What's he done, poor wretch?'

'N-nothing.' She looked up now and tried to smile. 'I was just a bit anxious, concentrating on getting everything down.'

He gave her the same glance of speculative amusement with which he had greeted her efforts to evade his questions about her singing. But all he said was. 'It's not my business. But have you two known each other before?'

'No,' she stated flatly. 'Did I give that impression?'

'No. He did,' replied Warrender, and he went out of the studio without further comment.

Kate returned to her office and, with a tremendous effort, contrived to shut out anxious speculations from her mind while she concentrated on her work during the rest of the morning and the early afternoon. Halfway through the afternoon Anthea looked in to say Sir Oscar decreed that she was to leave early. 'He says he doesn't require you and that you'd probably like to relax a bit before the performance.'

'Isn't it you and he who should do the relaxing?' Kate countered with a slight laugh.

'Oh, we shall,' Anthea assured her. 'But there's no reason why you shouldn't be free to savour the full pleasure of the performance. I hear it's your first visit to Covent Garden.'

'Yes, it is.'

'Lucky girl! I hope you enjoy it as much as I enjoyed my first visit there.'

'Was yours a *Don Giovanni*? and did Sir Oscar conduct?'

'No—to both of those. It was *Otello*, and I sat in a box with Oscar, nearly sick with mingled fright and rapture. It sounds so silly—but it was wonderful too.'

'It doesn't sound silly at all,' Kate asserted. 'It was a perfectly logical reaction. Did you know him then?'

'Hardly at all.' Anthea shook her head and smiled reminiscently. 'And yet I had the gall to ask him to wave to some student friends of mine in the amphitheatre!'

'And did he?' asked Kate with interest.

'You know, the extraordinary thing was that he did.' Anthea laughed. 'You wouldn't expect the lordly Oscar Warrender to *understand* the vital importance of such a thing, would you? Maybe that was when I first fell in love with him,' she added thoughtfully. 'Well, never mind about that now. Don't you fall in love with anyone tonight—and specially not with Carlo. He's a heartbreaker, but a bit of a scamp too. I hear you're going out to supper with him.'

'Yes, but I really can look after myself,' Kate assured her. 'Though I'm touched that Sir Oscar and you are so anxious for me to enjoy my evening,' she added sincerely.

'Maybe we're practising the uncle-and-aunt act for when the unknown niece arrives,' Anthea retorted with a laugh, and went away apparently without noticing that Kate caught her breath on a slight exclamation.

Back in her small hotel bedroom Kate spread out her evening dress on the bed and studied it

thoughtfully. It had been her mother's present—
her personal choice—and Mother had not always
displayed the best of taste, either in clothes or some
other matters. In this case, however, she must have
had a genuine flash of inspiration. The colour—for
which she had undoubtedly chosen the dress—was
a strange but beautiful sea green. ('A blonde's
green, darling,' she had said, and she had been
right.) And although she had lamented that it was
rather *plain*, the uncluttered lines could hardly have
been more becoming to Kate's really excellent
figure.

Unlike many of her contemporaries, Kate
believed firmly that a fine stage performance
deserved the compliment of a well-dressed audience—an audience obviously ready to take their
rightful part in an 'event'. No one would have described her appearance as magnificent, but no one
could have doubed that the girl with the beautifully
burnished fair hair, the dark-lashed grey eyes, the
faintly flushed high cheekbones, had gladly made
the best of herself in tribute to something she
expected to enjoy, heart and soul.

As she entered the crowded foyer of Covent
Garden and made her way to the ticket office it
did occur to her, with a frightful pang, that perhaps
the casual, thoughtless Carlo Ertlinger was capable
of forgetting his promise about the ticket. But she
need not have worried. The ticket was handed out
without comment and, as she made her way into
the beautiful auditorium, she saw that her seat was
an excellent one, on the gangway of the third row.

She studied her programme with some attention,

and was surprised to find that it gave her a strange
little thrill to see her famous uncle's name, and that
she experienced a rush of real affection at the sight
of Anthea's name.

The auditorium was filling up now and she
looked round with fresh interest. From one of
those boxes Oscar Warrender must have waved to
Anthea's humble friends in the upper reaches of
the house. From any one of these stalls——

And then her amused speculation abruptly
ceased, for as she glanced across the gangway
someone raised a programme in casual greeting,
and she realised that Evander Merton was sitting
almost directly opposite from her.

She hardly had time to return his salute before
the lights began to dim, the rustling ceased and a
moment later she saw Oscar Warrender making his
way through the orchestra to the conductor's desk.
Even her shock at the realisation of Evander
Merton's nearness could not quite stifle the unexpected feeling of pride and pleasure which she
experienced at the tumultuous welcome he
received. He was really nothing to her, she assured
herself. She was no more than his temporary secretary. And yet had she not come halfway across the
world in the hope of meeting him? and he was,
after all, the brother of the kind, clever, absentminded man who had married her mother and
provided her herself with a secure home and background. Suddenly she was overwhelmed by an
emotion which almost brought the tears to her
eyes, and only the first strains of the overture
recalled her to the realisation that Mozart, Oscar

Warrender and Covent Garden—in that order—
werè about to provide her with one of the great
experiences of her life.

Within minutes of Carlo Ertlinger's appearance
on the stage as the irresistible lover, Kate knew
why he had risen so rapidly to the top of the opera
league. She also thought she understood Sir Oscar's
reservations about him. The looks, the charm—
indeed the voice—were in no doubt. The musical
depth was not so certain. But that quality which
Warrender had described as animal magnetism
came over the footlights like an almost physical
force.

There was no question about his popularity with
the audience. And none about his awareness of his
own powers. Indeed, there was something extremely engaging about his sheer enjoyment of his
success, and this established a sort of rapport with
his public which many a more intellectual singer
might well have envied. Kate found herself surren-
dering completely to his remarkable combination
of gifts, and of the other artists on the stage only
Anthea, with her beautiful singing and her radiant
presence, had the power to take her attention from
the central character for more than a minute or
two.

By the first intermission she was ready to
applaud with the loudest. And it was a few minutes
before she realised that she was now right up
against the problem of meeting Evander Merton
once more and managing some sort of casual
conversation with him.

He came over to her as soon as the gangway was

comparatively clear and asked if she would like to come out for a coffee or a drink.

'Thank you, but I think I'll just stay here and look round,' she told him quite pleasantly. 'It's the first time I've been here, and I'm fascinated by the scene.'

He accepted that, but made no move to go. And suddenly, on a bold impulse she could never afterwards explain to herself, she looked straight at him and asked coolly, 'Did you find that missing photograph?'

'No.' His tone was equally cool. 'Did you expect me to?'

'No,' said Kate in her turn, and she realised that his short laugh had an element of admiration in it.

'You're a very interesting and surprising young woman, Miss Grayson,' he observed. 'If I ventured to ask you to come to supper with me after the performance would the answer again be "no"?'

'Unfortunately—and I mean unfortunately—it would have to be. I've already promised to go to supper with Carlo Ertlinger.'

This time he audibly caught his breath before he said, 'I told you you were an interesting and surprising girl, Miss Grayson.'

'You said "young woman", which was not quite so nice. And the name is Kate,' she replied, not quite sure whether she was making a desperate attempt to be friendly with a potential enemy or just responding to that light of admiration in his rather hard blue eyes.

'Kate,' he repeated, as though the one syllable held some sort of special significance. 'And I think

I told you that my friends call me Van.'

'Does that mean that I may?'

'The choice is yours,' he replied before he turned away.

'Thank you—Van,' she said to his retreating back, and she was nearly sure that he hesitated a second before he went on his way.

She opened her programme then and affected to study it, although she knew the work too well to need to refresh her memory on the action. Instead she stared unseeingly at the page and asked herself why she had behaved in that crazy way. The only answer she found was that perhaps she was tired of being forced on to the defensive, and that a little boldness might well combat any aggressive curiosity on the part of Evander Merton. Then she corrected herself. She had done nothing to parry his curiosity; all she could hope was that she had forestalled any aggressive *action* on his part. He was, she could tell, intrigued almost to the point of friendliness; and if she could keep him in that mood there was less danger in the fact that he was virtually certain of her real identity.

She gave him a brief smile as he returned to his seat across the aisle. And after that she had no difficulty in immersing herself in the performance again—right up to the tragic (and admirably staged) descent into hell by the now haggard though still handsome Carlo Ertlinger.

Without restraint she joined in the applause which greeted the appearance of the artists before the curtain after the performance. And when Warrender joined them she clapped extra hard, but whether in tribute to him as her employer or her reluctant uncle she was really not quite sure.

With some skill she contrived to mingle with quite a big party in her row and thus slip out without the necessity of any formal goodnight to Evander Merton. Then she went to consult a friendly cloakroom attendant on the best way of going round backstage.

'It's best to go out into the street,' she was told, 'and then round to the stage door, where you'll have to tell them who it is who's expecting you.'

She felt a little shy of claiming that the Don Giovanni of the evening was expecting her, so she just said, 'I'm Sir Oscar Warrender's new secretary.'

'Oh, then you won't have any trouble,' was the reply. 'Wonderful tonight, wasn't he? But then he always is. So is she—and a lovely lady to boot.'

Kate agreed to both expressions of opinion and then made her way round to the stage door, where the repeated statement that she was Sir Oscar's secretary gained her easy admittance. By careful observation and deduction she quite easily found the floor where the principal dressing-rooms were situated, but here she stopped in some dismay, for it seemed she was by no means the only one waiting for a few precious minutes with a favourite star. In fact, the narrow passage was crowded.

Doors opened from time to time to admit favoured visitors, dressers pushed past with stage costumes held high in their arms, snatches of song in what seemed stentorian tones at such close quarters sounded from some of the dressing-rooms, and over all hung that indefinable sense of excitement and triumph which indicates the successful conclusion of an important performance.

Feeling almost an intruder, Kate pressed back against the wall (which enabled at least three other people to press forward out of turn) and rather wished she had not come. Then suddenly the door immediately opposite her opened and Carlo stood there in the doorway in shirt sleeves, his dark hair curling damply on his forehead, and around him still the strange aura of the eternal lover doomed to self-destruction. Just for a moment something wrenched at her heart, and she could not have said whether it was pity or admiration. Then he smiled straight at her across the small forest of waving programmes and said,

'Kate! I thought you weren't coming. Come on in——' he jerked his head in the direction of the room behind him. Then he turned his smile on the autograph-hunters and said, 'Later, later—give me five minutes longer and I'll be with you all.'

She went in, the others falling back to make way for her, their curious, half envious, half congratulatory glances following her until he closed the door behind her. His dresser was still in the room, but that did not prevent Carlo from kissing her on both cheeks before he asked, 'How did you like it? How did you like *me*?'

In that moment she forgot what Sir Oscar had said about controlling her enthusiasm and replied, 'I thought you were perfectly marvellous. What else do you expect me to say?'

'I don't know.' He leaned back against the dressing-table and gave a curiously dissatisfied little laugh. 'I'm never sure how good I am until someone else tells me.—Am I, Robert?' he added, appealing suddenly to his dresser, who gave him a glance of mingled exasperation and affection.

'The whole audience have been telling you for the best part of the evening, haven't they?' he replied. 'What else do you suppose all that applause meant?'

'Oh, that——' Carlo shrugged discontentedly. 'They like the look of me, and the way I can leap about and swing a sword. The Maestro didn't fall over himself to tell me I was marvellous.'

'Sir Oscar? Ah, well, that's a different thing,' the dresser conceded. 'He's pretty sparing with his praise.'

'You're telling me!' Carlo laughed more easily that time. 'I shall leave it to you, Kate, to get out of him what he really thought.' And as he shrugged himself into his coat she remembered what her employer had said about being careful not to imply any excessive praise on his part.

'If he didn't tell you himself, I can't imagine he would confide any of his opinions to me,' she replied coolly.

'No?' Those dark eyes were suddenly very searching. 'You mean he didn't comment on me the other afternoon after I left the studio?'

'Not to me,' she said firmly, excusing the half lie to herself with the reflection that he had not *volunteered* any comment; he had merely answered her direct question.

Carlo accepted that, called a friendly goodnight

to his dresser and ushered Kate out of the dressing-room into the midst of the patiently waiting fans. She had to admire his technique with them. He was good-humoured, patient in his turn, and somehow able to give the impression to each one that he or she was the person he most wanted to meet. Even when the performance was repeated at the stage door Kate could not quite decide whether it was good technique or a good heart which prompted this highly successful way of dealing with his public.

When they were free of the admirers at last he ushered her into his car, which he drove himself, and took her off to a small but very elegant restaurant where he was obviously well known. Only then did she realise that he was slowly but quite deliberately beginning to relax from a state of great tension.

'It's a tough job being a successful singer, isn't it?' she said, smiling across the table at him.

'It's like walking a tightrope,' he agreed. 'You're on trial at every single performance. I wouldn't want to be anything else myself now. It gets you like a drug. But I don't think I'd advise anyone to start on it if they weren't already committed.'

'Wouldn't you?' She looked startled and he asked quickly,

'Why do you say it like that? Don't tell me you have ambitions yourself.—Though, now I come to think of it, I did notice you had some talent the other afternoon.'

'*That?*' Kate could not hide her scorn. 'That wasn't the best I can do.'

'No?' he looked amused and suddenly rather curious. 'Tell me just what you mean by that, Kate. Do you mean that you were nervous, which would be understandable—or deliberately doing less than your best, which would be intriguing?'

'Oh——' she was dismayed to find she had stumbled like this upon the forbidden subject, but she realised that she could not risk leaving him to do some dangerous guessing on his own account. So she said slowly, 'I'd like Sir Oscar to hear me one day, but in better circumstances. I wasn't in any way prepared that afternoon.'

'Fair enough,' he agreed. And then, on what was obviously a goodnatured impulse, he added, 'Would you like me to mention it to him and get you a proper audition?'

'Oh, no, no!—thank you.'

'Why not?' Carlo set that handsome mouth rather obstinately.

'Because——' She stopped and then, with a sudden surge of excitement, she thought, 'Why not, indeed?'

'It wouldn't be difficult for me to make an opportunity,' he assured her carelessly. 'I suppose Warrender would buck like a startled horse if his secretary suddenly turned round on him and claimed to be the coloratura he'd been waiting for——'

'The middleweight lyric,' she interjected almost absently.

'The middleweight lyric,' he repeated, accepting the correction. 'But if I said that I'd persuaded you to talk about yourself and I thought it might be worth his while to hear you, he might well look down that handsome nose of his and go through the motions of objecting. But it just isn't in him to resist the faint, faint possibility that he had a singer of some quality right on his own doorstep, so to speak.'

'You think so?' She tried to keep the light of excitement out of her eyes and failed.

'I do. Especially if you look all starry-eyed like that.'

'I don't want him to bother about my starry eyes,' she replied impatiently. 'I want him to notice my voice.'

'Both have their attractions, Kate,' he assured her, and reached for her hand.

Inoffensively but with some skill she avoided his touch, however, and at that he laughed and said, 'Enough of the Don Giovanni act for tonight, you mean? Well, you're right, I suppose.' And then, with an abrupt change to almost boyish weariness, he exclaimed, 'Oh, God, I'm so *tired*!'

'Well, here comes your supper,' she told him gently. 'You're hungry as well as tired, I expect. Eat that now and don't feel you need to make conversation. Then you go home for a good night's rest.'

'Dear Kate! I won't insult you by telling you that you sound positively maternal. But you're restful—how strange! I don't think I've ever known anyone restful before.'

She made no answer to that, though she could have told him it was not a quality that most women would imagine he required. Instead, she addressed herself to her own delicious meal and from time to time cast a half-amused glance at her companion, who now seemed more like a hungry schoolboy than a dazzlingly successful stage artist.

At last he looked up, met her eyes and said, 'Thank you, dear Kate.'

'For what?' she asked with a smile. 'It's I who should be thanking you. For a memorable performance, a charming meal—and the offer to get me an audition with Sir Oscar. And incidentally, I accept that offer. Only please don't speak to him until I give you the word. I must find a studio and put in some concentrated practice before he hears me. I haven't had much opportunity to sing recently.'

'All right. Do you know of a good studio?' Carlo sounded totally professional all at once. 'You don't? No, I remember—you said you hadn't been here long. This is the place you want.' He scribbled down an address on a page of his diary, tore out the page and pushed it across the table to her.

'You've spoiled your diary!' she exclaimed, for she noticed it was a handsome one.

'No.' He smiled straight at her. 'I've left a gap which will always remind me of the most important evening of the year.'

The smile did odd things to her, even though she assured herself she must not take him seriously. Indeed, she said drily, 'If you use that line with lots of girls you must have a rather depleted diary.' And she liked him very much for the fact that he laughed heartily and made no attempt to protest.

He insisted on taking her home, even though she

suspected it was a good way from his own hotel, and because of that she felt she could not evade the kiss he gave her as they said goodnight.

'I know where to find you now,' he said with an air of satisfaction as he glanced up and noted the name of her unpretentious hotel. But, grateful though she was for her evening and his offer with regard to Sir Oscar, Kate decided it was not incumbent upon her to tell him that in a few days' time she would be moving to a small furnished flat she had found.

The next morning both the Warrenders asked her how she had enjoyed the performance—Anthea with real interest and Sir Oscar with rather perfunctory politeness.

'I thought you were both magnificent and I was proud to know you,' she replied without hesitation. 'I'd never experienced a performance anything like that before. Where I come from——' she stopped, and Sir Oscar glanced at her keenly and said,

'Yes? Where *do* you come from, as a matter of interest?'

She thought for moment that her heart had stopped. Then it went racing on again and, to her astonishment, she heard herself say quite coolly, 'From the other side of the world, which means I was never near a big opera house. Last night was about the most exciting night of my life, in more ways than one.'

'She means she went out to supper with Carlo,' observed Anthea with an indulgent laugh, and Kate, seizing on the diversion, said, 'Well, that was pretty exciting too. He was good, wasn't he, Sir Oscar?'

'Not bad,' Warrender conceded, and then he added musingly, 'It's odd, you know, but the most utterly convincing Giovannis are often peasants offstage and yet grands seigneurs when the magic of the performance is upon them. The great Ezio Pinza was like that. I heard him just once when I was no more than a schoolboy, and I've never forgotten it.'

'You did?' exclaimed Anthea. 'You never told me about it.'

Immediately she and Warrender were lost in operatic reminiscences and comparisons, and Kate felt that the moment of danger was past. Indeed, after a few minutes, she was able to say quite casually, '*Is* Carlo Ertlinger a peasant offstage, as you say?'

'Yes. I'm surprised he didn't tell you so,' Warrender replied. 'He's half proud of the fact and half resentful of it too, which produces a sort of bravado in him that is sometimes excessively irritating and sometimes oddly touching.'

'I know what you mean,' said Kate, suddenly remembering that moment when Carlo stood in the doorway of his dressing-room.

'I believe his father was of good solid peasant stock, and his mother an impoverished beauty from quite an old family. It's an interesting mixture. You never know where God's going to put a voice,' he added, half to himself, as though musing pleasurably on the ever fascinating subject of the human voice.

Then Anthea said, 'Oh, your friend Evander Merton was at the performance. Did you know?'

Resisting the impulse to retort that he was no friend of hers—for, after all, had she not last night half acknowledged him as a friend?—Kate replied coolly, 'Yes, I did. He sat quite near me and we exchanged a few words.'

'He came backstage,' Anthea went on, 'and had a chat with us. Oscar says he's an unusually knowledgeable young man, which is a blessing if he's going to do this book. He seems to haunt the Garden and other centres of music, so no doubt we shall be running into him from time to time.'

'No doubt,' agreed Kate. And then, as that sounded a trifle bald, she added, for something to say, 'Does he sing himself?'

'No, fortunately,' put in Warrender, who was examining his post. 'Apparently he's an accomplished pianist, however, and has even done some professional accompanying from time to time.'

And there the subject of Mr Merton and his musical accomplishments rested.

During the next few days Kate's life ran smoothly. She was interested in almost every aspect of her work, and she made the transfer to her small furnished flat with the minimum of trouble. With her few personal treasures now unpacked and around her she felt almost at home, and began to think seriously of the need to get herself into good vocal form if she were to avail herself of Carlo's offer before it should slip from his mind.

There was, of course, no piano in her small flat, so that intensive practising was virtually impossible, and she decided that on the very next free afternoon which came her way she would go to the address Carlo had given her and see if a studio were free.

Her employer, who was a demon for work when work was required, had an unexpectedly indulgent streak in him where legitimate relaxation was concerned. He never kept Kate to the grindstone just for the sake of doing so, and it was not unusual for him to let her go early if there were no real work for her to do. Consequently, she only had to wait about a week before finding herself with a free afternoon, and the immediate opportunity to spend a couple of hours at the studios recommended by Carlo.

The girl at the reception desk told her that she would have to wait about twenty minutes, but Kate rather enjoyed watching the coming and going of students and some obvious professionals. She found the atmosphere familiar in a subtly exciting way, and suddenly she thought how long it was since she had been able to devote herself to her true ambition. How had she borne the almost total separation from the study and endeavour which had been for some years her whole life?

At that moment she was summoned to the desk and told that a studio was available.

'It's one of the best and biggest ones,' the girl told her in a friendly tone. 'It's your first visit, isn't it?—I thought I hadn't seen you before. Well, go up those stairs to the first floor, turn left along the corridor to Room 15. And don't forget to bring me back the key when you leave.'

Kate followed the instructions and was a little surprised to find that Room 15—one of the best and biggest—was quite a small room. But the sight of a piano at last, and the sense of being totally alone and free to indulge herself in full-throated song made her overlook any shortcomings in the room itself.

She was a sufficiently good pianist to be able to accompany herself reasonably well and, having tried out a few scales and one or two specially effective exercises which her excellent teacher had taught her, she was surprised to find how full and round the voice sounded.

'It's partly the smallness of the room,' she told herself, but she knew perfectly well that her voice was in remarkably good shape. A little out of practice she might be, but the enforced rest seemed to have enhanced the voice rather than reducing it.

Kate spent a wonderful hour. With the recollection of the *Don Giovanni* performance so fresh in her mind, she sang one of Zerlina's arias, wondered what it was like to play that role on the stage— opposite Carlo Ertlinger, for instance—and then went on to one or two of the Italian romantic roles.

She refrained from pressing the voice too far, but towards the end of her hour she allowed herself the indulgence of the big soprano air from Cilea's *La Wally*, and then she sat there at the piano wondering if it were really as good as it sounded to her.

She stared down at her tightly clasped hands— and only then did she catch sight of her watch and realise that she was dangerously near the end of her time. Hastily gathering together her things, she snatched up the key from the piano and hurried to the door. It stuck slightly, then came open with a suddenness which gave her a slight shock. But that was nothing to the shock she experienced as she stepped out into the corridor.

For there, a few yards away, stood Evander Merton, regarding her with an expression of complete astonishment.

CHAPTER THREE

FEELING like a burglar caught with the silver inadequately concealed, Kate stared speechlessly at Evander Merton, who simply asked curtly, 'Who was that singing?'

She thought for a wild moment of brazening it out—of pretending there had been someone else with her in the studio. But one glance of those cold blue eyes warned her not to try any such feeble invention.

'If you mean—who was singing the *La Wally* aria, I was,' she stated defiantly.

'You extraordinary girl!' He came a step nearer. 'That's a very remarkable voice you have. Has Warrender heard it?'

'No. At least, not when I was singing full voice. I—I just filled in for Zerlina one afternoon when he was taking Carlo Ertlinger through the second act.'

'You just filled in for Zerlina,' he repeated incredulously. 'Isn't that something? And two days later you were pinching family photographs, and the following evening you went out to supper with Ertlinger after one of his best triumphs. You really have been living it up, haven't you?'

'Is any of this your business?' she managed to ask coldly.

'Perhaps not. But it's extremely intriguing,' he

countered. 'It might even put an extra page into that book I'm writing.'

'You wouldn't be so *mean*!'

'I might,' he assured her carelessly. 'Come out to tea with me and we'll talk things over.'

'I don't want——' she began, then she glanced down at the key in her hand and exclaimed, 'Oh, I must give this back. I'm over time already.'

As she started down the stairs she realised that he was still beside her. He paused with her at the desk and coolly accompanied her out into the street where he summoned a passing taxi. When she would have left him he put a hand lightly round her arm and said pleasantly, 'No, no—I insist.' And, short of an unseemly struggle, Kate had no choice but to obey the pressure of his fingers.

'Is it of any interest to you that I don't *want* to come and have tea with you?' she asked with suppressed fury as the taxi started with a jerk that flung her against his arm.

'Not much,' he replied. 'Did your mother never tell you there's no stopping a determined journalist when he—or indeed she—is on the trail of a good story?'

'What do you know of my mother?' The startled, angry question slipped out before she could stop it.

'Quite a lot, as it happens,' he told her coolly. 'My sister was very nearly the plaintiff in a libel action against her.'

'Oh, no!' Kate's hand flew to her lips in a gesture of dismay.

'Oh, yes,' he assured her. And then there was

complete silence until they arrived at the Ritz and, still wordless, she preceded him into the tea room. Then, as she sat down opposite him, she said almost fiercely, 'Well, what are you going to do about it?'

'My dear!' he laughed protestingly. 'This isn't the second act of *Tosca*. Nor am I interested in a spot of blackmail. I am, however, genuinely curious to know your mother's version of that near-libel incident back in New Zealand. How much do you know of the story, Kate?'

For a moment she was tempted just to tell him to mind his own business. But apparently the fact was that that embarrassing chapter in her family history *was* partly his business. He, of all people, had been personally concerned.

With a slightly trembling finger she traced the pattern on the tablecloth. Then, without looking up, she said, 'I was away at boarding-school at the time—in my last year. I knew that my mother did journalistic work. I—I was rather proud of her. She told me about some of the genuine successes she had——'

'In scandal-sheets?' he enquired.

'Am I telling this story or are you?' Her coldly contemptuous glance made him blink.

'My apologies. Go on.'

Kate swallowed nervously, and then went on slowly, as though painfully recalling each detail, 'When I came home for the holidays I realised that some crisis had occurred. Mother was in a state of acute nervousness. She even cried a lot, which wasn't like her. She refused to answer any of my questions, and my stepfather told me—sternly for him—not to worry her. There were some very uneasy days, and then suddenly it was all over. I remember that evening quite well. I remember she said more than once to my stepfather, "Denis, how did you do it? Whatever did it cost you?" and he said, "Not as much as it was worth to see you happy again." He was like that.'

'So you never knew the real story?'

She shook her head and he asked drily, 'Would you like to hear it now?'

'You mean your version of it?' She curled her lip. But as he fell silent she suddenly knew she wanted passionately to hear what he had to say. So she added casually, 'You can tell me if you like.'

'No—if *you* like,' he replied, throwing the onus on her without any attempt to help her. And after a moment she said huskily, 'Tell me, then.'

'It was nearly five years ago, so you probably won't recall that at that time there was a pretty unpleasant scandal about a very prominent public man and a young woman who was no better than she should be. Her name was Julie Martin.'

He paused and Kate said uneasily, 'It—it seems to ring a bell.'

'Your mother secured what might be described as a pretty ripe interview with the lady and sold it to the kind of newspaper which deals in such stories. Unfortunately, the accuracy of the article was not equal to the picturesque terms in which it was couched. The name was given as Julia Merton, which happens to be my sister's name and—by what I'm sure your mother would regard as a piece of malignant fate—she happened to be staying in a furnished apartment in the same block.'

'Oh—how *awful*!'

'For your mother—or my sister?'

'I was thinking of both,' said Kate not absolutely truthfully.

'I don't need to describe the fury in my family, the exchange of lawyers' letters, the frantic recall of as many copies of the rag as possible——'

'You were personally concerned in all this, of course?' She gave him a glance of mingled despair and dislike.

'Of course. I was on the spot. And if it had been *your* sister, what would you have done?'

'I know—I know. I do understand. At least, I think I do. But it's in the past now. It's *over*,' she said almost pleadingly.

He made a slight grimace of acceptance. And then he said, 'Since we're delving so far into the family background—I take it that you are of course the niece Warrender has no intention of having in his home?'

'He wouldn't describe me as his niece,' Kate retorted. 'To him I'm just the daughter of the woman his brother married.'

'Of the woman who married his brother would, I imagine, be more accurate,' he corrected gently. And he was agreeably startled by the way her eyes flashed at him.

'Oh, I know it's all too easy to make snide remarks about people like my mother!' Kate's voice shook slightly. 'In many ways she is a silly woman, and her taste isn't always of the best. But, if you must know, she and my stepfather loved each other dearly——'

He started to make some apology, but she swept on furiously.

'My own father was an engaging scamp, I imagine, and Mother couldn't have had a day's security during his lifetime. My stepfather gave us both a happy and secure home. He wasn't intimidating, like Sir Oscar. He—he was a darling.' She bit her lip but, though she paused, he made no attempt to interrupt her this time, and presently she went on,

'I don't think he ever guessed my mother had rather desperate designs on him when we met on board that ship going to New Zealand. He just thought how gay and warm and loving she was— which in a sense was quite true. He couldn't believe his luck when she agreed to marry him. And *she* was stunned by his sheer goodness and his generosity. He solved every problem she had, and he loved her to the day he died. It may sound just a cheap, sentimental story to you, but——'

'It doesn't sound that way at all,' he said, with unexpected seriousness. 'It sounds rather touching—and true. I'm sorry I baited you about it.'

Kate cleared her throat, took an absentminded sip of her tea and then said, more calmly, 'Well, are you going to tell Sir Oscar all about this conversation?'

'No.'

'Why not?'

'Because it isn't my business. At least the bit

about your relationship to him isn't. What does interest me personally is the matter of your voice. It really is outstanding, you know. I could tell that even through the door. For heaven's sake, don't you *want* Warrender to know about it?'

'Not until I'm in better form. I've been travelling a good deal during the last seven or eight months, and I'm out of practice. Today was the first time I had a chance of some serious work since I came to this country. And even then I had to play my own accompaniment, which made it——'

'I'll play for your practising if you like,' he interrupted.

'*You* will?' She was astounded as she reflected on the harsh words they had been exchanging only minutes ago. 'But why?'

'Because I'd like to and because I'm a qualified accompanist. I've done quite a lot of professional work in my time and I keep in practice. That's why you ran into me at the studios. I go there two or three times a week. I don't doubt Warrender is capable of judging a voice of quality in any condition, but you're right to want to be in good form when he first hears you. Then when you're ready I should like——'

'No,' she interrupted him quickly. 'I'll be glad to accept your offer of the accompanying—if we can make some proper working arrangement, I mean— but when it's time for Sir Oscar to hear me Carlo has already offered to speak to him on my behalf.'

'Ertlinger?' He made a slight face. 'You don't want to put yourself under an obligation to a fellow like that.'

'He's a good friend of mine,' she replied coldly.

'Really?' He looked annoyingly sceptical. 'Well, then I won't attempt to tarnish his halo. Of course he's very exciting and attractive and all that. But he's a bit of a bounder, you know.'

'No, I don't know,' retorted Kate, still in that chilly tone. 'And come to that, why should I put myself under an obligation to a man like *you*? You haven't been specially nice to me.'

He looked unexpectedly taken aback at that and said, 'I'm sorry, Kate,' which surprised her.

'And I'm sorry, Van,' she replied, which surprised her even more. Then they both laughed rather ruefully and she said, 'Don't let's quarrel. I truly appreciate your offer to play for me sometimes when I practise. Strictly on a business basis, of course.'

'What exactly do you mean by that?' he wanted to know.

'Well, naturally I should expect to pay a professional accompanist for his or her services.'

'You needn't plan on paying me,' he stated shortly.

'Then I can't accept the arrangement,' she replied impatiently. 'You must see that. And please don't start arguing about it. I don't *want* to argue. I'd rather be friends, Van.—Wouldn't you?'

She held out her hand to him across the table and, after an appreciable pause, he took it without comment. She would have liked to ask him why he hesitated, but he called for the bill just then, and she had no time for questions until they were outside on the pavement. Then she summoned the resolution to ask, 'Why did you hesitate just now about taking my hand?'

For a moment she thought he was not going to reply, then he said, 'Because, I suppose, I have a nasty suspicious streak in me. A little voice at the back of my mind enquired, "Was that a real gesture of friendship on Kate's part? or was it a clever move to disarm me?"'

'Oh,' she said, and that was all.

'Aren't you going to tell me?' he asked persuasively.

'No,' she replied. 'You don't deserve that I should.'

Then, as a bus stopped at the traffic lights, she jumped on, called from the platform, 'Goodbye, and thanks for the tea,' and was borne away, while he stood and looked after her with a smile that was half angry and half intrigued.

During the next few days Oscar Warrender kept Kate very busy. He and Anthea were to go to Paris the following week for a concert and there were several matters to be cleared up before their departure. On the other hand, he told her she could take things easily while he was away.

'Look in each day and go through the post,' he told her. 'Deal with anything within your province and phone Dermot Deane if you have any queries. Then if there's nothing requiring your immediate attention you can leave after lunch and occupy yourself in your own chosen way.'

'As a matter of interest,' put in Anthea, who happened to be in the room, 'what *is* your favourite way of spending your spare time?'

Kate started to say something about exhibitions and galleries, but Warrender, without looking up from the letters he was signing, said, 'She sings. She's going to brush up her singing technique if she's a sensible girl.'

'How do you know?' Kate stared at him, her cheeks very pink.

'It's my business to know these things,' he told her. And although he smiled, it was not the kind of smile which encouraged further questions.

The moment she was alone Kate telephoned to Carlo Ertlinger's hotel and was lucky enough to find him in. He was obviously very pleased to hear from her, but she cut short his greetings by asking pointblank, 'Carlo, have you said anything to Sir Oscar about my singing?'

'No. Should I have done so? I thought you wanted me to keep quiet until you gave me the go-ahead.'

'I did,' Kate said. 'But he *knows*. I mean, he knows I'm interested in singing, and even teased me a little about brushing up my technique while he's away in Paris. Now how did he know about that?'

'There isn't much Warrender doesn't find out if he wants to,' Carlo laughed. 'Who else knew besides me?'

'No one.—Oh!' She stopped suddenly and caught her breath. Surely Van Merton would not have betrayed her confidence so callously? True, the secret of her voice was not the most dangerous of the things he knew about her. But if he could be unscrupulous about that he might well take a malicious pleasure in dropping other damaging hints.

'Are you still there?' Carlo's voice enquired. 'You are?—Well then, when am I going to see you again? Indeed, when am I going to hear you sing, Kate? You say you're going to brush up your voice while Warrender is in Paris. Suppose I meet you at the studios one afternoon and——'

'Oh, no!' She had a momentary and rather horrifying vision of Van and Carlo meeting head-on. 'That wouldn't do. I just don't know yet what I shall be doing next week. I'll phone you.'

'Well, don't try to put me off too often,' he warned her laughingly. 'Jealous baritones can be dangerous fellows, remember!'

The following Monday morning Kate found herself in sole charge of the Warrender office, a situation both gratifying and intimidating. She was determined to give a good account of herself, and was all the more put out therefore to be confronted almost immediately with a matter about which she knew absolutely nothing. After some thought she finally followed the advice Sir Oscar had given her and telephoned to Dermot Deane.

'Hm—well, there's only one person who can give you the background of that particular business,' he told her, 'and that's Isobel Caterham.'

'But she's still in the nursing home,' Kate objected. 'I can't very well bother her.'

'Oh, yes, you can,' Dermot Deane assured her. 'She's getting on well and is probably bored to tears by now. She'll be flattered to be consulted. She reckons there isn't much about Warrender's affairs that she doesn't know as well as he does. And damn well right she is too,' he added reflectively. 'You go and see Isobel.'

So, having cleared off a few routine matters during the morning, Kate went along to the nursing home that afternoon, with a sense of lively curiosity. Aware that it is well to tread tactfully in the footsteps of a highly qualified predecessor, she made no secret of her genuine admiration for Miss Caterham's magnificent office routine from which she had herself benefited so materially, and Miss Caterham was not displeased to receive the tribute.

'One does one's best, of course,' she said, being aware in her turn that 'one' in that context is so much more telling than 'I'. 'What can I do for you? Dermot Deane telephoned to say you had some problem.'

Kate explained, and was almost awed by the speed and ease with which her predecessor recalled every detail of the situation and offered the solution with the finesse of a master chef producing a delectable cake.

'Thank you,' said Kate with sincere gratitude. 'I know what the Warrenders mean when they say you are irreplaceable.'

Miss Caterham received this further tribute with a deprecating little laugh, but her tone was friendly—almost intimate—as she said, 'Now *you* tell *me* what happened over that book Evander Merton was going to write. Did Sir Oscar agree to be in it?'

'Yes, he did.' Kate gave her a few details of the

progress so far, and then added on a sudden impulse, 'Do you know him, Miss Caterham?'

'I've met him,' was the nicely judged reply. 'He's quite a good accompanist, you know. He once accompanied a young friend of mine who thought—mistakenly—that she had a professional voice. I felt rather sorry for him.'

Kate, who had never had any reason to feel sorry for Evander Merton, suppressed a smile and asked curiously, 'What's your opinion of him?'

'As an accompanist?—very musical and quite sensitive.'

'I meant more—as a person. Would you think him trustworthy? a man of integrity and——'

'I shouldn't otherwise have advised Sir Oscar to have anything to do with him or his book,' was the shocked reply. 'I don't think you need worry about that aspect.'

'I won't,' said Kate, abandoning any idea of extracting a less Warrender-orientated opinion. 'I'd better go now before I tire you.'

She stood up as she spoke, but was arrested by Miss Caterham's suddenly adding, 'I think perhaps Evander Merton is a rather *hard* man, with a lively contempt for anything second-rate. Just as well, of course, if he's to write about Sir Oscar. Apart from that I think it would be unwise to antagonise him.'

'I should say you're right,' Kate agreed grimly, and she took her leave.

As she made her way out she was astounded to come face to face with a young nurse conducting— of all people—Carlo Ertlinger along the corridor.

'Hello! What are *you* doing here?' As she

stopped, Kate took in at one glance the pink cheeks of the young nurse, the careless charm of Carlo, and the magnificence of the bouquet he was carrying.

'The same as you, I imagine.' He switched his dazzling smile from the nurse to Kate. 'Visiting Isobel Caterham. (Thank you, Nurse—I know my way now.)' He gave the nurse a pat on her shoulder and she trotted away in a happy daze.

'I never thought of your visiting the sick somehow,' Kate said candidly. 'Or of your knowing Miss Caterham particularly well either.'

'Anyone wishing to make the grade with Warrender is wise to get to know Isobel pretty well,' he replied with equal candour. 'Though, to tell the truth, this is a visit without an ulterior motive. I'm genuinely fond of her. She was very kind to me in my earlier days and got me out of an awkward scrape with a catty prima donna who shall be nameless.'

'You don't say!' Kate laughed. 'I'm continually learning new things about you. Nice things,' she added, for she found it oddly touching that the sought-after Carlo Ertlinger should find time to take flowers to the quite unglamorous Miss Caterham.

He smiled as though a little puzzled and then asked, 'Are you on your way back to the Warrender apartment?'

'No. I have the rest of the afternoon free.'

'Then wait for me, Kate, in the waiting-room.' he exclaimed persuasively. 'I shan't be above fifteen minutes. Then we'll go to the studio and you shall sing for me.'

'Oh, I don't know——' she began.

'Well, I do!' There was a sudden flash of almost boyish temper. 'For heaven's sake stop saying "no" to everything I suggest. I shall begin to think you dislike me.'

'All right—all right.' Kate was surprised to hear how indulgent her own laugh sounded. 'I'm sorry. And there's no reason why you shouldn't hear my voice, of course. I can play for myself.' Resolutely she pushed the thought of Van Merton from her mind. 'Take your time. Miss Caterham will be pleased to see you, and I wouldn't cut short her ration of glamour by one minute.'

'Oh, she doesn't think I'm a bit glamorous, you know,' he said quite seriously. 'She thinks I'm an irresponsible but nice boy who needs good advice from time to time.'

'She could be right at that,' Kate retorted amusedly. Then she went into the palatial waiting-room.

She counted it to Carlo's credit that he kept her waiting a little longer than he had said, and she dismissed his apologies with the sincere observation, 'I think it was nice of you to let her feel you had all the time in the world for her.'

His car was waiting outside and in that they drove to the studio. Obviously he was known there, and the receptionist regarded Kate with speculative, if discreet, interest as she handed her the key to the room she had previously occupied.

'What are you going to sing for me?' Carlo enquired as Kate sat down at the piano. 'I'm sorry

I don't play well enough to accompany you. But anyway, I want to watch you as well as listen.' And he picked up a chair, turned it and, with a sort of careless grace, straddled it. Then he leaned his arms on the back of it and regarded her with the utmost attention.

If anyone else—Van Merton, for instance—had done that Kate supposed she would have been rather put out. With Carlo she felt no selfconsciousness at all. His frank interest was such that she forgot about his being a famous artist and, almost without reflection, she began to play the opening bars of Manon's aria from the second act.

'*Adieu, notre petite table*,' she sang, softly, regretfully and with genuine pathos—right through to the end, with the half-stifled sob.

'You like singing that, don't you?' said Carlo. 'It's lovely, but you make it almost too tragic—too sad.'

'She *is* sad, though! She's truly sorry to be deserting Dex Grieux.'

'Think so?' He shook his head sceptically and laughed. 'She would have preferred him to be the one with the money, of course. But when it came to choosing between him and the gay life she didn't hesitate. But you're entitled to your own interpretation, of course, and the voice is beautiful, Kate. I wish I were a tenor,' he added impatiently. 'We'd do the Church Scene from *Manon* and make you take fire. What is there we could do together? The poor old baritone doesn't get much of a look-in with the soprano, operatically speaking.'

'Giovanni and Zerlina?' she suggested.

'Oh, no! Zerlina never takes fire. She doesn't even smoulder, calculating little baggage that she is. Do you sing Nedda?'

'Ye-es. But again the hero is a tenor, isn't he?'

'She's only *married* to him. It's Silvio she loves.'

'Oh, yes, of course. I'd forgotten.'

'Never forget Silvio, darling. Nedda couldn't forget him, remember.' His voice took on an almost caressing note. 'That's why two people are murdered. He's the classic example of the irresistible, troublemaking chap from village life, the kind who always awakens the bored young wife of the elderly husband. I've seen it again and again——' He broke off, and then said with curious intensity, 'I *feel* for Silvio. He didn't really plan to make trouble, he just followed his animal instincts. Dangerous, of course, very dangerous,' he added regretfully. And Kate thought she heard him say, 'I should know!' under his breath.

'And what motivates Nedda?' Kate asked, curiously fascinated by his ability to turn stage characters into people one might meet every day.

'Nedda?—who knows? Boredom with her husband, sentimental reaching for some sort of romance in a dreary world, possibly even a genuine and passionate love. Let's try the duet together and find out, shall we?'

He laughed and, getting up from his chair, came to stand beside her at the piano. For her part, Kate was suddenly strangely excited and very faintly scared, though she was not sure why. She picked out a note or two on the piano and said, 'I'm just trying to remember how it goes——'

'Take it from here.' He leaned across her so that he was unexpectedly close, and sketched a phrase or two.

'Yes, I've got it!' She began to play, and all at once that warm, seductive baritone voice was addressing her personally in a melody which had captured the world long before she was born.

Good musical discipline made her join in accurately at the right point. But then something she had never before experienced warmed and coloured her voice with a sort of sensuous excitement that was totally alien to Kate Grayson, and entirely in keeping with the infatuated Nedda. She *had* to respond, she *had* to let Silvio know that she loved him and, casting all her humdrum life aside, would go with him.

The beautifully blended voices soared to a triumphant peak and came to a stop. And at that point Carlo picked her right up in his arms and kissed her several times—laughing, breathless and in some curious way exultant.

'You see?' he said, still holding her close against him. 'That's how it should be done! You're learning, my little Kate—you're learning!' And, as she disentangled herself from his embrace, she was nearly sure that he was referring to something other than just singing.

Afterwards, she was to look back on that session with Carlo as something between a piece of magical nonsense and a really valuable lesson. If, in addition, there was a spice of danger—that was part of the charm of the occasion, and she kept any real awareness of it at the back of her consciousness most of the time.

Only when they finally left the studio and came downstairs to the reception desk did something happen which shook her out of her euphoric mood.

'A note for you, Miss Grayson.' The girl at the desk handed her an envelope and Kate, as she preceded Carlo into the street, slid her thumb under the flap, abstracted the sheet of paper and—idly and then incredulously—read the very firmly written contents.

'I'm sorry you didn't let me know this afternoon was a practising session,' the note said. 'I should have been happy to make good my offer to accompany you—though possibly the presence of a third person would have made the *Pagliacci* duet less convincing. No prizes, I presume, for guessing the identity of the promising baritone singing with you. Yours—Van.'

She gave a slight gasp, which made her companion glance at her and ask, 'Something interesting?'

'No, nothing of any importance whatsoever,' she replied, and crumpled the note and thrust it into her pocket. But when Carlo tried to persuade her to join him for tea or cocktails she refused almost abstractedly, bade him a rather short goodbye and went home to her flat, where she flung herself into a chair and said aloud, 'Of all the unutterable cheek! What makes him suppose——?'

The ring of the telephone bell interrupted her, and she stared suspiciously at the instrument, trying to recall which of her few London acquaintances even knew her telephone number. Then, with angry suspicion in her heart, she snatched up the receiver and said, 'Yes?' in an unpromising tone.

'This is Van Merton,' she was not surprised to hear. 'I thought perhaps——'

'How did you get my number?' she demanded, before he could develop his thoughts.

'Lady Warrender gave it to me,' was the cool reply.

'Lady War—? I don't believe it. Why should she?'

'She suggested I should keep a friendly eye on you while they were away,' he informed her calmly. 'She seemed to think—Are you still there?'

'Yes, I'm still here,' Kate assured him grimly. 'I'm just more or less speechless at your cheek, and the poorness of your invention. Why on earth should Lady Warrender suggest that *you*, of all people, should—what was it?—keep a friendly eye on *me*?'

'I suppose she took me to be a fairly reliable sort of chap.' He sounded quite unmoved by her scornful incredulity. 'Anyway, she said——'

'Don't bother to tell me any more of what she said—or didn't say. I think you're telling me a pack of impudent lies,' Kate told him angrily. 'And, incidentally, if that silly note you left for me this afternoon is part of your hamfisted idea of *keeping an eye on me*, you can just think again! I'm not your affair, Mr Merton. I have no wish to be considered your affair. And as for your impertinent reference to accompanying me when I'm practising—I'd rather accompany myself on a tin whistle than avail myself of your offer!'

There was a slight pause. Then he said, 'It's pretty difficult to sing and accompany oneself on a whistle at the same time. Had you thought of that?'

She had, as a matter of fact, just before he said the words, and was annoyed to find she had some difficulty in suppressing an hysterical desire to giggle. She controlled the impulse, however, and said coldly,

'I don't think we have anything more to say to each other. Except that, from something Sir Oscar said, I realise that you must have gone tattling to him about my singing and——'

'I did nothing of the kind!'

'——about my singing,' she repeated ruthlessly. 'And about some other things too, I shouldn't be surprised to hear. I don't like you, Mr Merton. I don't trust you. And, incidentally, you bore me to distraction.'

And on this splendid valedictory speech she hung up the receiver with a slightly trembling hand.

Only then did it occur to her that both she and Isobel Caterham had agreed that Van Merton might be a dangerous man to antagonise. And so during the next few days she alternately congratulated herself on the crispness of her repartee and deplored her lack of basic caution.

On the morning after the Warrenders' return from Paris Kate arrived at the apartment in a state of nervous tension which she had some difficulty in concealing. Anthea had brought her a charming scarf from Florian, the famous dress house, and greeted her kindly. But, even so, this hardly seemed the moment to ask, 'Did you suggest to that pushing Van Merton that he should keep an eye on me?'

Sir Oscar enquired about several matters which had cropped up while he was away, and seemed to approve of the fact that she had consulted Miss Caterham over the one thing beyond her own capabilities. Nothing in the manner of either of the Warrenders furnished the slightest clue to Evander Merton's ridiculous claim, and Kate had almost managed to consign him to the category of 'unimportant details' when, halfway through the morning, her employer glanced up and said,

'Have we heard any more about Merton and his book?'

Kate gulped slightly. 'No—nothing about the book.'

'Well, he may be a slow worker, for all we know. We haven't had much experience of him yet.'

Kate, who felt she had had all too much experience of Evander Merton, was suddenly goaded into unwise speech. Turning from the filing cabinet where she had been standing, and ignoring the fact that her employer was obviously immersed in his own affairs, she blurted out the one question she was longing to ask him.

'Sir Oscar, has Evander Merton ever talked to you about me?—about my—my personal affairs, I mean?'

'No.' He made a note or two on the page in front of him. 'Does he know anything about your personal affairs? And, if so, has he any reason to suppose they would interest me?'

She was shaken, but now she had to blunder on.

'For one thing, you knew about my—my singing interests. I don't know who else could have told you.'

'No?' He did look up then, leaning back in his chair and regarding her without favour. 'It didn't occur to you that I might be able to draw my own conclusions, without recourse to Mr Merton's aid?'

'You mean—you guessed for yourself?'

'I mean that I guessed for myself.'

Kate had a terrified impulse suddenly to ask what else he had guessed for himself. But she swallowed down the words and just stood looking back at that cold, handsome, intelligent face which had been the inspiration—or the terror—of many artists over the years.

Then Warrender almost negligently held out his hand to her and said, 'Come here.'

CHAPTER FOUR

SLOWLY Kate crossed the room and took her employer's outstretched hand. She was half frightened by the strength of the fingers which closed round hers, half fascinated by the slightly sardonic smile with which he regarded her.

'Well, Kate,' he said. 'I take it you are the so-called niece?'

She nodded wordlessly. Then after a moment she found sufficient voice to whisper, 'How long have you known?'

'Oh, quite some time.'

'Then why didn't you send me away?'

'For one thing, you were proving a very good secretary,' he told her realistically, 'and a good secretary was what I badly needed at that moment. For another——' he considered that—'I suppose the situation intrigued me. Any more questions?'

She shook her head.

'Then you shall answer some questions for me. How did you and my brother get on?'

She was astonished by the sheer personal interest of his tone, and she replied without hesitation, 'I loved him. I think he loved me too. He was so kind and generous—and reassuring. Quiet, of course, and almost unassuming. But life was so *secure* when he was there.'

'He was not much like me,' Oscar Warrender

said musingly.

'Oh, *no*!' Kate agreed with such emphasis that he smiled drily and said, 'Your point is taken.'

'I'm sorry.' She blushed scarlet. 'I didn't mean that as a criticism. It was just——'

'I understand. Just a comparison not particularly in my favour. I'm not hurt. Did he ever speak about me, Kate?'

'Yes.' She hesitated. 'He had a great regard for you, and said more than once that you deserved all the fame and success that had come your way. But he added——' she hesitated again and Warrender said, 'Go on.'

'He said that your greatest piece of good fortune was to marry Anthea—to marry Lady Warrender. That if you hadn't done so you would have become a very hard man and perhaps a lesser artist.'

She was silent, and so was he for a moment. Then he said slowly, 'He was perfectly right, of course—yet he never met her. How did he know that, I wonder?'

'From your letters, I think.'

'But I hardly ever wrote any!'

'He said once that you wrote one about six months after you married, and that told him all he needed to know.'

'You don't say!' He laughed and, for the first time in her knowledge of him, flushed slightly. 'I wouldn't have credited him with so much human perception.'

'Oh, but he was *clever* as well as a darling!' Kate exclaimed.

Warrender did not query that. He merely said,

after a moment's pause, 'You'd better go and tell Lady Warrender about the new state of affairs.'

So Kate went away in search of Anthea, and found her in the drawing-room, completely immersed in something she was reading. Without even looking up, she asked absently, 'Does Sir Oscar want me?'

Kate regarded the lovely creature Oscar Warrender had married and then laughed and said, 'I think he always wants you, doesn't he?'

Anthea did look up then and say with a smile, 'Well, that's a nice thought.' Then she added curiously, 'What's happened? You look both excited and anxious.'

'I suppose I'm both,' Kate admitted. 'Sir Oscar says I can tell you I'm what he describes as the so-called niece. Which makes me a sort of niece of yours too. I hope you don't mind.'

'My dear girl!' Anthea jumped up and kissed her. 'I'm charmed—and not especially surprised. Oscar suspected it from quite an early stage, but I wasn't entirely convinced. Enough though to feel faintly responsible for you and even to ask that nice Van Merton to keep an eye on you while we were in Paris. Did he do so, incidentally?'

'He—tried to.' A sense of something like dismay chilled the joyous warmth of Kate's mood. 'Though it wasn't really necessary, you know.'

'No, perhaps not,' Anthea admitted. 'But I knew your people were somewhere on the other side of the world. And, as being an aunt is a new experience for me, maybe I overacted. I'll get used to it! Now come and tell me more about how you gatecrashed into our lives.'

So Kate sat down on the sofa beside her and explained about her ambition to meet her famous uncle, her diffidence about any claims she might have to being a worthwhile singer and how, consequently, she had made a slight change in her name and presented herself as the well qualified secretary she had managed to become.

'It seems a bit complicated,' Anthea said good-humouredly. 'But go on. Was Dermot Deane in the plot?'

'Oh, no!' Kate was shocked. 'I wouldn't have involved anyone else. I just wanted to make sure that when—*if*—Sir Oscar heard me he wouldn't have any—any prejudices beforehand.'

She could not bring herself to mention her mother, and Anthea avoided the delicate topic also. She merely said warningly, 'Don't pitch your hopes too high, Kate. Oscar is a difficult person to please, vocally speaking. And the fact that you are a sort of relation would make him more, rather than less, strict. Particularly——' she made a slight face—'if you revert to your real name of Olga Warrender.'

'That *isn't* my real name,' Kate exclaimed earnestly, and then she flushed slightly. 'That was a bit of fantasy on Mother's part. My real name is Katherine Olga Gray. But, though I was never actually adopted, Mother was keen on my being called Olga Warrender, because—it sounds silly, I know, but——'

'It's all right,' Anthea said kindly. 'You mean that it had a certain likeness to Oscar's famous name. Don't apologise. Lots of people like to add a bit of vicarious glamour to their lives and names. There's no real harm in it, Kate. Though don't tell Oscar I said so,' she added with a little grimace. 'You'd better go on calling yourself Kate Grayson. It's pretty and it suits you. As for the way you address us—I'm happy to have you call me Anthea, but I don't think "Uncle Oscar" is quite right for the Warrender image, do you?'

'Oh, no!' Again Kate was genuinely shocked, which rather amused Anthea. 'And there's certainly no reason to emphasise any relationship. It can remain an absolute secret if Sir Oscar prefers that.'

'Hm——' Anthea looked reflective. 'A well-kept secret is one thing, but a secret which leaks out can have some awkward repercussions. I can think of at least three ill-wishing sopranos who would be ready to say, "She's no niece of his! She's his *daughter*," if only to embarrass and annoy me.'

'Oh!' Kate looked appalled. 'I never thought of that.'

'Oscar did,' said Anthea without rancour. 'He brought it up the first moment we began to suspect you might be the niece. But don't look so horrified. We've weathered the odd bit of scandal in our time. People in our position have to. It's seldom that anyone dares to needle Oscar himself, of course, and I'm thicker-skinned than I used to be.'

'Would you rather I just took myself off?' Kate asked earnestly.

'No, of course not! Don't be silly,' replied Anthea equably. 'I only wanted to warn you, so that you avoided actually asking for trouble. I suggest you simply go on being Oscar's nice, efficient secretary until Isobel is ready to take up the reins again; then we'll play it from there.'

'You're being very kind and generous.' Kate bit her lip. 'And I promise not to impose on the situation in any way.'

'I know, my dear.' Anthea touched her arm reassuringly. 'Anyway, as you know, we're pretty busy people, with a good deal of coming and going throughout the musical world. We shan't be exactly treading on each other's toes. Of course I shall always be very happy to see you, Oscar too,' she added, with rather more haste than conviction.

'Thank you,' said Kate. 'But—but if it *should* turn out that I have a voice of some quality, wouldn't that bring me into Sir Oscar's orbit in a rather personal way?'

'Oh, well——' Anthea coughed slightly and Kate thought she had only just checked herself from saying how remote that possibility was. Then, before Anthea could frame any real reply, her husband came into the room, glanced keenly from one to the other, and asked a little drily,

'Well, are all the revelations completed?'

'More or less,' Anthea assured him. 'We've decided that Kate should keep to the present version of her real name and continue as your secretary until Isobel Caterham is ready to return. Meanwhile she will sometimes call me Anthea, to indicate a more informal relationship, but will continue to address you as Sir Oscar. We don't think it's necessary to make any reference to a special connection between you and her.'

'You seem to have covered most aspects of a

tricky situation.' He smiled a trifle grimly.

'Except——' Kate began impulsively, and then she glanced rather appealingly at Anthea.

'Speak up for yourself,' Warrender commanded her. 'You'll never get anywhere—as a singer or anything else—unless you can show some resolution when it's needed.'

'It was about my singing that I wanted to speak to you,' Kate told him as firmly as she could. 'I was hoping you would hear me some time and—and give me a candid opinion.'

'Oh, no, my dear,' he assured her cynically. 'My candid opinion is almost the last thing most of you want to hear. A gasp of wondering admiration is what you're counting on. But that isn't the way it works, Kate. So far you've done little to convince me that you have the determination and drive essential for even a modest success in the world of the theatre. You lack the elbows, as the German saying has it.'

'But I *am* determined—I *am* willing to work and struggle,' she insisted.

'Yes, that's what you all say. But you have been here—what is it? some weeks—and you have never yet summoned up the guts to ask me to hear you. Why?'

'She's asking you now,' Anthea interjected softly, but he took no notice of the interruption.

'It wasn't lack of courage—at least, not entirely so.' Kate faced him with sudden defiant resolution. 'But it was obvious to me that you don't suffer fools gladly, and I would have been a fool to try to sing to you before I was in good vocal form. I did tell Carlo Ertlinger, because he guessed I had a voice, and we decided to wait until—I mean, he offered when the right time came to use his influence with you——'

'He has no influence whatever with me,' Warrender assured her coldly.

'Well then, he offered to speak to you on my behalf—to tell you that he'd heard me and found me not untalented, and to ask if you would hear me yourself.'

'You had only to make the request personally,' Warrender told her drily. 'I will hear you this afternoon at three o'clock.' Then he turned and went out of the room, leaving Kate shaking with mingled excitement and fright.

'Oh——' she gasped to Anthea—'do you suppose he really means it?'

'Yes, of course he means it,' Anthea assured her. 'But don't think you're over the fence yet. You're just coming up to it.'

'Oh, I know, I know! And thank you for all your help and support. Thank you even for asking that interfering Van Merton to keep an eye on me,' Kate added with an excited little laugh. 'Only don't encourage him any further,' she said, a dash of caution cooling her flame of gratitude. 'He's already too managing by half. In fact he infuriated me and I'm afraid we exchanged some hard words.'

'Did you?' Anthea looked regretfully amused. 'Well, make it up with him if you can. I rather like him. And I really love the way he's handled the first chapters on Oscar.'

'But they haven't been delivered, have they?'

Kate looked surprised. 'Sir Oscar was commenting on their non-appearance only this morning.'

'He sent them direct to me, by special messenger,' Anthea explained. 'People often do that sort of thing,' she added elliptically; meaning, presumably, that she was easier of approach than her intimidating husband. 'He asked me to read them and hand them on to Oscar if I approved of them. Do you want to look through them?'

'I'd love to! If you think Sir Oscar wouldn't mind my seeing them before he does.'

'I don't know why he should. He has other things to think about. Take a quiet hour to look at them, it'll relax you. Then go and have a light lunch and half an hour's practice at some studio away from here. I presume you know of a studio to go to? If not——'

'Yes, I know one,' Kate assured her. 'But Sir Oscar might think I was slacking—even imposing on the new situation—if I just take myself off like that.'

'No, he would expect you to relax a little before an important audition. I'll go and tell him. If he has anything really urgent he knows where to find you.'

'Well, if you really think it's all right——' Kate flipped over the pages in her hand and said curiously, 'I wonder why Van Merton sent these to you rather than direct to Sir Oscar.'

'I suppose he felt a bit diffident about his work.'

This sounded so unlike anything Kate knew of Mr Merton that she found nothing to reply. Instead, she took the manuscript across to the window-seat and sat down to read it, although she hardly thought anything would distract her from her own concerns at this juncture.

She was aware that Anthea went out of the room, and then put in her head a few minutes later to say, 'Sir Oscar doesn't need you and says you're to take things easily until three o'clock, when he'll expect you in his studio.'

'Thank you,' Kate replied almost absently, for she was already completely absorbed by the manuscript in her hand, hardly able to believe that the brash, self-assured Van Merton could have written anything of such subtlety, warmth and perception.

Had she herself been asked to describe what she thought Oscar Warrender had been like in his youth she would have had to say that she had no real idea. But Van Merton *knew*! The arrogant, attractive, dedicated creature who emerged from the typewritten pages was the young Oscar Warrender to the life. More important still, one could already trace the beginnings of the great conductor he was to become.

She read through to the end. Then she put down the pages and stared out of the window, enthralled and yet somehow dismayed by what she had read.

So *that* was how Van Merton wrote! There must be far, far more to him than the provocative, abrasive figure she had constructed in her own mind. The writing was extraordinarily sensitive, which meant—reluctantly she had to concede it—that he must have a certain sensitivity himself. Something which had been conspicuously absent from any of *her* dealings with *him*.

She bit her lip as, with great clarity and some distaste, she recalled a few of the things she had said during that ill-fated telephone conversation, and with almost passionate intensity she wished them unsaid. At the time she had thought them smart and telling; now they seemed rather silly and juvenile. At the time she had thought herself utterly indifferent to Van Merton's opinion of her. Now she realised that, surprisingly, it meant a great deal to her. She no longer wanted to be at odds with him. She wanted—as she herself had said in a moment of greater awareness—to be friends with him.

At the time he had asked if she really meant that, and she had prevaricated because she had not really known the answer herself. Now she knew, beyond any question.

'So where do I go from here?' she muttered to herself, stirring uneasily in her corner of the window-seat. Was there any way back from the situation she had herself created?—short of humbling herself in a way that would be almost unbearable. Her pride cringed at the thought. But then suddenly pride did not seem of paramount importance. If she told him——

Already she began to form a few promising sentences in her mind. Then she glanced at the clock, realised it was much later than she had supposed, and recalled with something like shock that Van Merton had actually displaced from her mind the immense fact that she was to audition for Oscar Warrender that afternoon.

Hastily slipping on a coat, she went out for the

recommended light lunch—though when it came to the point, she found she had very little appetite for it. Then she walked the short distance to the studios, telling herself with something between hope and alarm that there was more than a slight possibility that she might find Van there.

There was no sign of him in the entrance hall, and she had to force herself to ask the receptionist as casually as possible if he had been there.

'He's upstairs now,' was the reply. 'If you can wait a few minutes, he should be down quite soon.'

Kate said she would wait and took her seat on a bench in the hall. She felt excited and very nervous, and told herself this was because of the coming audition with Sir Oscar. To some extent this was true, of course. But to an even greater extent she was nervous at the thought of encountering Van, and each time the lift doors opened she swallowed a maddening lump in her throat, and rehearsed her opening sentence.

And then, when he came, she completely forgot what she had planned to say to him. She just stood up and took an impulsive step towards him. He glanced at her passingly, then walked on as though she were invisible, threw his key down on the desk and went out by the swing doors into the street.

She simply couldn't believe it! If he had said something bitter or insulting she could have understood it. That he should totally ignore her was like a blow in the face, and for a moment she could only stare after him in stunned dismay. Then, indifferent to any appearances, she ran after him,

caught up with him on the pavement and said
breathlessly, 'Van!'

'What do you want?' He turned and regarded
her as though she were some unwelcome stranger
importuning him.

'I—I——' Then a breath of inspiration made the
words tumble out. 'Van, I need you. Sir Oscar is
going to audition me this afternoon, and I desperately need half an hour's practice. Will you *please*
play for me, as you promised?'

'No,' he said quite deliberately. 'I have neither
the time nor the inclination. I suggest you go and
play on your own tin whistle.' And he brushed past
her and went on his way.

It seemed to her that she stood there in the street,
staring after him, for some minutes. It could not
have been long really, but she was beyond measur-
ing time, or indeed deciding what she was going to
do next. She began to walk along aimlessly, trying
to reconstruct the shattering scene, asking herself
where she had gone so hopelessly wrong. Then she
wondered why she had supposed he would react in
any other way. She had grossly insulted him only a
few days ago—and then asked him to do her a
favour. Why *should* he play for her just because
she had suddenly found an opportunity to sing for
Warrender?

Then, with a shifting of emotional gears that was
like a physical shock, the recollection of the precious audition blotted out everything else. The audition! and here she was, some distance from the
studios, with no practice accomplished, and no
time now to go back and repair the omission. Not

even the most perfunctory run-through of whatever she proposed to sing was possible.

'Then I just can't sing for Sir Oscar,' she told herself despairingly. 'I can't, the way I'm feeling now.'

Self-pity threatened to overwhelm her. But then she recalled with painful clarity Warrender's contemptuous assessment of her powers of resolution and the will to work. She had been offered this great chance. She had come halfway across the world in the hope of just such an opportunity. And now, because of a few contemptuous words from Evander Merton—*who was nothing to her*, she insisted—was she to creep back and say she didn't feel like singing after all, thank you?

'I should *deserve* his contempt if I did that,' she told herself. And resolutely she made her way back to Killigrew Mansions and the studio where Sir Oscar would be waiting for her.

In point of fact, he was not actually waiting in the studio when she arrived five minutes early. But Anthea was, and asked with real interest if she had managed to run through whatever she proposed to sing.

'No,' said Kate with desperate frankness. 'The— the time was too short after all.'

'A pity,' said Anthea more coolly than she usually spoke. 'I wouldn't volunteer that information to Sir Oscar if I were you. He likes people to get their priorities right.'

Kate was tempted to say that it had not been quite her own fault, but she judged that neither of the Warrenders would have much interest in feeble excuses. Certainly not where professional standards were concerned. It had been her *business* to be as well prepared as possible for the important audition. Any failure to do so was a black mark against her, even in the eyes of the usually sympathetic Anthea.

Sir Oscar came in just then, and Kate almost physically braced herself for the ordeal.

'Relax,' said her uncle as he passed her on the way to the piano. 'You can try a simple scale to begin with.'

Relieved that this at least had required no last-minute polishing, she sang full voice, clearly and with great musical accuracy.

'Good,' he said once, as he took her further and further over an extended range, and then he asked her what exercises she did.

Less nervous now, she explained, and he made her try out familiar ones and a couple that were new to her. Then he asked, 'What are you going to sing for me in the way of an aria—song—oratorio number? whatever you like.'

Kate said that she would sing the aria from *Manon* which she had sung for Carlo. Warrender immediately began to play the music leading up to it, and then paused to say, 'Take your time, but don't make it dreary. Her regrets are real but not profound. She's sorry to ditch him—but other things will matter more.'

It was that last explanatory remark which suddenly stirred Kate's emotions most painfully. Not unlike the situation between Van and herself. She was sorry to have ditched him—but she hoped other things would matter more. Only—would they?

'You're not paying attention!' Warrender struck a sharp chord. 'Don't let your thoughts wander. You're Manon, remember, not Kate Grayson pretending to be Manon. Go back to the beginning.'

So she went back to the beginning and tried to repress all thought of Van. The result was that she kept her emotions so rigidly under control that when she permitted herself the slight sob at the end, it came out with heartbroken emphasis and she found there were tears in her eyes and then—shamingly—actually on her cheeks.

'Stop that nonsense,' Warrender said without sympathy. 'Either stop crying and learn to sing, or sob your heart out and give up singing. It isn't possible to do both.'

'I—I'm sorry,' stammered Kate. 'I didn't mean——'

'She's nervous,' murmured Anthea protestingly.

'Of course she's nervous,' returned Warrender impatiently. 'Every performer is nervous at times. I am myself occasionally.'

'Are you, darling?' said Anthea. 'Don't ever let me know or I'll go to pieces.'

He laughed at that, touched her cheek with unexpected tenderness, and then fetched Kate a glass of water.

'Drink that and cheer up,' he admonished her. 'You've got a good, healthy voice to which nothing wrong has ever been done. You can thank your teacher for that. It's unawakened, of course, in the way so many voices are today. Very pleasant, not one really horrid sound—and no earthly reason why one should want to hear it again. It's at this point that the work begins, and the question is—what is the owner going to do with that voice. Ready to try again?'

Kate said she was. But at that exact moment they all heard a quite prolonged ring at the front door bell and, glancing at his wife, Warrender asked impatiently, 'Are we expecting anyone?'

As Anthea shook her head, the maid knocked and came in.

'It's Mr Ertlinger, sir,' she said. 'He wants to know if you'll see him.'

Before Warrender could answer either way Carlo walked in with the kind of smiling assurance that few people used in Warrender's presence. Then he stopped short, seeing Kate beside the piano, and exclaimed, 'Hello! What's going on here?'

'If it interests you,' Warrender told him unsmilingly, 'I am trying out Miss Grayson's voice, and I'd rather not be interrupted.'

'But of course it interests me!' Carlo declared with his most winning smile. 'I came to see you about this very matter. What did she sing for you?'

'She made a sketchy attempt at one of the *Manon* arias. We were about to try it again, and if you can keep quiet for ten minutes you may sit down and listen.'

'Oh, but I implore you—don't waste time on the *Manon*. She isn't very good in that,' stated Carlo with candour. 'Have you heard her as Nedda?— You haven't? Then let her do the Nedda and Silvio duet with me. That's what I've come about.'

'I don't follow,' Warrender said coldly.

'No, I was just about to explain.' Carlo bestowed a smile on Anthea and Kate and then came back to Warrender with a more serious expression. 'I'm in a spot,' he asserted engagingly. 'Francesca Poli wants to be released from her part in the Charity Gala at the end of the month. We were doing the Silvio–Nedda duet together, and now she's opting out. I want you to let me have Kate instead.'

'You must be mad!' Warrender stared at him in genuine astonishment. 'The girl has never been on a professional stage.'

'She doesn't need to have done so,' Carlo stated easily. 'This is a concert. She only needs to put on her prettiest dress and let me lead her on to the platform, and I'll do the rest.'

'How do you mean—you'll do the rest? Do you propose to sing both Nedda and Silvio?' asked Warrender ironically.

'No.' Carlo laughed, his good humour quite unruffled. Then he added persuasively, 'Wouldn't you like to hear Kate and me do the duet?'

'Not specially,' was the blunt reply. 'But if she wants to do so——?' He glanced interrogatively at Kate.

'Yes, please!' The colour rushed into her cheeks. 'I want to very much indeed.'

Warrender shrugged and went to the piano.

'Stand there, where I can see you both,' he ordered, and they moved unhesitatingly into his line of vision.

Kate's heart was pounding with excitement and a kind of wild hope. Could they bring off that marvellous rapport again? Could they inspire each other with the same exultant, romantic emotion? She simply did not know until she heard Carlo's first phrases uttered in those warm, beguiling tones. And almost immediately she once more seemed to slip into the identity of the passionate, loving Nedda. Nothing else mattered. All she had to do was to keep sufficient control to make her voice do what she wanted. In a strange way, the rest—as Carlo had boastfully declared—could be left to him.

After the last triumphant notes, Warrender turned to his wife and said, 'What do you think?'

'It's a calculated risk,' replied Anthea.

'Yes, it's a calculated risk. With the emphasis on the risk,' he agreed. Then he turned back to Kate and Carlo, who stood hand in hand, looking rather naïvely expectant. 'Can you do that more or less to order?' he asked curiously.

'Yes,' said Carlo.

'I think so,' said Kate.

'And you want to try?' This time he addressed only Kate.

'Yes,' she said resolutely, 'I do.'

'Very well, then. I will give you all the help I can,' said Oscar Warrender.

CHAPTER FIVE

'THIS isn't really happening to me,' Kate told herself once during the next hour. But only that once did she allow her thoughts to wander from the detailed instructions which Warrender was giving her. Even Anthea, though she remained in the room, made no attempt to comment unless her husband specifically sought her opinion.

To Kate's initial surprise, Sir Oscar dealt very little with the actual duet which it was proposed to use at the concert. What he made her reflect on with the utmost attention was the whole role of Nedda.

'You don't just start being Nedda at the beginning of the duet,' he informed her. '*You have been Nedda* since the opera began. Indeed, if you are an artist of any sensitivity you became Nedda some while before that—even in the dressing room.'

'I would suggest——' began Carlo, but Warrender interrupted him.

'You will suggest nothing,' he stated drily. '*I* am giving Kate this lesson. Granted that you stirred her emotions to a fine pitch originally. But that's not going to sustain her when the romantic bubble bursts. She'll need much more behind her performance than thrills of personal excitement.'

'But I think——' Carlo got up and came towards the piano.

'Sit down,' said Warrender without raising his voice. 'You can make your observations later.' And Carlo sat down immediately, looking rather like a chastened schoolboy.

At the end of the lesson Warrender allowed them to sing the duet again, and Carlo said discontentedly, 'She did it better the first time.'

'Of course she did,' replied Warrender, unmoved. 'But she is beginning to build a real foundation now, and is trying to combine some fresh discoveries with her instinctive knowledge. Eventually she will do it a great deal better than that first attempt.'

'If you say so——' Carlo shrugged sceptically.

'Yes, I say so.' Warrender smiled without offence. 'And now—you've played your part very well and can take yourself off on your own affairs.'

'But these *are* my own affairs! I'm waiting to take Kate home.' The young baritone looked both surprised and affronted.

'No,' Warrender assured him, unmoved. 'Kate has one or two things still to do in the office. She is my secretary as well as your artistic partner, you may remember. She has also quite a lot of work to do on Nedda before we team you up again. If she's really to join you at the Charity Gala, she has to do us both credit, and I don't intend her to have a superficial idea about professional requirements. You can join her for another lesson at—let me see——' he consulted his diary—'at three o'clock on Friday afternoon.' And, with good-humoured but quite resistless authority, he wafted young

Carlo Ertlinger towards the door.

Kate wanted to laugh. But she was also a shade disappointed, for she would have liked very much to thank Carlo adequately for his magical intervention in her affairs, and to discuss with him further the whole question of the Charity Gala.

But, like Carlo himself, she had no technique for opposing Sir Oscar's authority. She *was*, as he had said, his secretary and subject to his requirements. So she gave Carlo a quick, regretful smile as he took his leave, and then went to the office to await her employer's instructions.

It was ten minutes or so before he rejoined her, and when he came, there seemed little that he required of her. Two hours ago Kate would not have dreamed of querying anything he did or said, but, with new confidence in herself, she said with a smile, 'You just didn't want to have Carlo take me home, did you?'

'That is correct,' he agreed. 'Ertlinger is by nature a charming time-waster. In the ordinary way, if you chose to waste time with him that would be your business. But not if you've undertaken a stiff professional task under my direction. You might type those two letters for me and post them as you go. Otherwise you're finished for the afternoon.'

'Except for the boundless gratitude I want to express,' she said earnestly. 'I can't tell you——'

'Then don't try,' he interrupted her. 'The one form of gratitude I require from you is a hundred per cent dedication to the task of making that duet something people will remember and talk about.

Carlo has his part in the enterprise—we'll make no mistake about that—but he is not able to provide more than a unique emotional excitement. That can be a very important element, of course, but no worthwhile career has been built on emotional excitement alone.'

'You say—a worthwhile career,' Kate ventured shyly. 'Do you mean that I just might have that?'

'Too early to say. It is, as I said, a good voice which is basically well produced. But that isn't much more than saying that a gifted pianist owns a splendid piano. It's a means to an end, and that end can be either glorious or disappointing. It's up to you. You understand?'

'Yes,' said Kate humbly, 'I understand.'

Then she turned to the two letters, typed them with painstaking accuracy and, when he had signed them, took them with her to post on her way home.

Just as once before she had left that same flat so excited that she simply had to walk in order to give some vent to her feelings, so she turned into the Park now and went past the seat where she had sat on that previous occasion. Or rather, she would have gone past it if someone had not risen from it and said, 'Kate! I've been waiting for you.'

'*You* have?' She stared up in resentful astonishment at Van Merton. 'But why? I thought you—you'd indicated that we had nothing more to say to each other.'

'But I have something to say,' he said doggedly. 'I want to say I'm sorry.'

'For what?' She clasped her hands tightly together and looked down at them so that she would not have to look at him. 'I deserved what you said.'

'No, you didn't.' He took the clasped hands suddenly and drew her a little towards him. 'Will you come and sit down for a minute or two and let me explain? Or,' he added with quite uncharacteristic humility, 'have you not got the time?'

'I have time,' she told him, and she went with him to the bench where he had been sitting. If she noticed that he still held one of her hands she said nothing. Nor did she make any attempt to withdraw it. Only, after a short pause, she said, 'What did you want to explain?'

'It—it isn't really an explanation. More an extended apology. Kate, I know I have a tendency to fly off the handle—to show a temper I don't always control as I should. I was pretty raw over some of the things you said on the phone; they weren't quite justified, you know——'

'I know now. And I'm sorry too.'

'Not with so much reason. But it wasn't only that. I was ridiculously tense and nervous this afternoon—anxious about something personal that meant a lot to me. You see, I had that morning submitted the first pages of my study of Sir Oscar and——'

'Oh, I know! I've read them. They're simply marvellous!'

'You've *read* them?' He almost literally fell back from her. 'But how could you?'

'Lady Warrender let me see them. She thinks

they're splendid too, and I think she felt she simply had to show them to someone else, only Sir Oscar was busy. I couldn't have believed that you—that anyone,' she corrected herself quickly, 'could have written so knowledgeably, so convincingly about him. It's as though you'd *known* him at that time.'

'Well, I had, in a way.'

'But you couldn't have!' Kate did some quick mental arithmetic. 'You wouldn't have been more than a schoolboy then.'

'That's just what I was.' His blue eyes sparkled suddenly and there was a dash of colour in his cheeks. 'It sounds corny, I know. Just a bit of hero-worshipping. But it was much more than that. He came to my school when I was—oh, I don't know—ten maybe, and he talked to us about music. I've never forgotten it. It was like someone throwing open windows on an unknown world. I knew from that moment that music must be a part of my life. He spoke of what it meant to him personally—a young conductor just coming into the world class—and it was more exciting than anything I'd ever read, because I *knew* what he was talking about. He was a bit of a show-off, of course, very arrogant, very good-looking. But none of that mattered. About his music he was quite humble.' Van paused and then he said simply, 'It was like a revelation.'

'But, my dear—but, Van—didn't you *tell* him that was how you came to be interested in writing about him? He couldn't be anything but pleased and flattered.'

'I didn't want him to be pleased and flattered.

At least, that wasn't the main idea. I wanted him to judge my work on its own merit, and feel that I'd written correctly about him. I could tell him later how I came to know him. Later—or nor at all,' he added half to himself. 'It didn't really matter.'

'But of course it matters—a lot,' Kate declared. 'And I understand now why I was completely riveted by those early chapters. So much so that I actually forgot that Sir Oscar had agreed to audition me—Oh!'

'Yes,' he said ruefully, '"Oh!" indeed. Kate, I'm so truly sorry. No anxiety or nerve-strain can justify what I said to you. Please forgive me.'

'It's all right.' She smiled at him almost shyly. 'Forget it and let's start again.' And it occurred to her that she had seldom enjoyed a sentence more.

'Thank you.' Again there was that unfamiliar note of humility. 'And now dare I ask how the audition went?'

'Of course you can! It went well.'

'You mean Warrender was genuinely impressed?'

'No, I wouldn't quite say that.' Kate laughed. 'He said I had a good healthy voice to which nothing wrong had ever been done. But that it was an unawakened voice—I think he meant boring—and everything from now on depended on what I did with it. Then he gave me what amounted to a lesson on the spot, and he put more into an hour's instruction than most people would have managed in a week.'

'I don't doubt it. Is he going to give you

other lessons, Kate?'

'I think he is.' Suddenly she was cautious, for she did not want to tell him about Carlo's part in the afternoon's events. She had an uneasy feeling that some sort of cloud might then descend on the brightness of their new-found friendship. 'There's some faint chance that I might do something semi-professional, but I'm not to say anything about it at the moment. Nothing is settled.'

'Well, that's splendid!' Van looked so intrigued that she was relieved to remember there was another subject she might mention.

'Oh, Van, Sir Oscar guessed that I was what he calls his so-called niece. And he doesn't mind much—and Lady Warrender doesn't mind at all.'

'I didn't tell either of them anything about it, you know,' he said a little defensively. 'I certainly never betrayed any confidence of yours.'

'I know. And it doesn't matter now. Lady Warrender——' she cleared her throat—'confirmed the fact that she'd asked you to—to keep an eye on me. And,' she stated more confidently, 'I told her it had been quite unnecessary.'

They both laughed then a little selfconsciously, and Kate added, 'Apart from the Warrenders and myself you're the only person to know the connection between Sir Oscar and me. For the time at any rate we would all prefer to have it remain a secret.'

He said that of course he understood, and that he must not keep her any longer now, as he had noticed her shiver a little in the keen wind.

It was so novel to have Van Merton concern

himself with her wellbeing that she smiled and said, 'It was worth being a bit chilly in order to straighten things out. I'm glad, Van.' And she held out her hand to him.

'I'm glad too,' he replied as he took the out-stretched hand. 'And this time I'm not going to ask if this is a gesture of genuine friendship or simply—whatever nasty crack I made before.'

'You don't need to. It's genuine friendship,' she told him. 'And, Van, does this mean a renewal of your offer to play for my practising sometimes?'

'It certainly does! Just tell me the time and I'll be at the studios.'

'Is early evening any good to you? My daytime hours do really belong to Sir Oscar.'

'The day after tomorrow, about six-thirty?' he suggested, and she nodded agreement.

'Oh, and Van, Sir Oscar is letting me do some work on Nedda.'

'Apart from the famous duet?' he enquired quizzically.

'The——?' She was startled at first and then remembered that he had overheard her trying the duet with Carlo at the studios. 'Not only the duet,' she said hastily. 'Sir Oscar thought it was a part I might study.'

'Really?' he looked impressed. 'It's a demanding role for a beginner. If that's what you really are.'

'Oh, Covent Garden isn't bidding for me yet,' she assured him lightly. 'It's just that I've always liked the role and Sir Oscar says that if I'm going to study it I must do the job thoroughly. And now I really must go.'

They stood up and for a moment she thought he was going to offer to accompany her. But then, with a tact which surprised her, he bade her goodbye and let her go on her way alone.

Hardly had she reached home when the telephone bell summoned her, and when she picked up the receiver she was not surprised to hear Carlo's voice say, 'That brute Warrender kept you pretty late, didn't he? I've tried you twice before this.'

'There were one or two things to be done—and he *had* given up most of his afternoon to me,' Kate reminded him. 'But, Carlo, I'm so glad to speak to you, and to thank you over and over again for you wonderful help.'

'It was rather a miraculous intervention, wasn't it?' he agreed, with an engaging lack of false modesty. 'Not that I was responsible for the timing. That was a nice bit of work on the part of fate. I believe in fate, Kate—do you? Fate, luck, strange timing—whatever you like to call it. I believe, for instance, that it was a bit of fateful juggling that brought you and me together at the right time,' he added solemnly.

'Well,' said Kate lightly, 'that's a pleasing theory. Carlo, had you *really* come to suggest to Sir Oscar that I should sing with you at the Gala?'

'Not really—no,' he admitted reluctantly. 'It was for something else, rather unimportant. But when I walked in and saw the scene all set—you near the piano and Warrender getting ready to play God— I had the sudden inspiration, and couldn't resist combining my dilemma with your great chance. And it came off, didn't it?'

'It certainly did,' she agreed, but a trifle uneasily. 'It was a great risk, though. Are you sure you truly want *me* to sing with *you* on a big occasion? I'm just a nobody, vocally speaking, you know.'

'No, you're not. You're my discovery, darling. Not Warrender's, incidentally. And you and I are going to do a lot of things together, Kate. You'll see! I have plans for us, but don't ask me about them yet—they're not complete. I'll be seeing you on Friday, my love, and don't let Warrender bully you too much between now and then.'

She heard him replace the receiver. But his charm and confidence seemed to linger in the room, and Kate sat there for some minutes, smilingly reviewing the incredible events of that afternoon and speculating enjoyably on the real meaning of Carlo's last words.

From that day onwards Kate's life changed. Not that her relationship with her famous uncle became markedly different. She was still very much the secretary to the busy conductor, and if he ever thought about their tenuous family connection nothing in his attitude towards her showed it. But for half an hour—sometimes a full hour—on most days he found time to supervise her vocal studies.

When she told him that Van Merton was going to accompany her for some of her practice sessions he nodded approvingly and said, 'Well, he's a knowledgeable fellow, but don't let him take over. Make him understand that I'm in charge so far as real instruction is concerned.'

'He does understand,' Kate assured him earnestly. 'But he is talented, isn't he? Those first chapters about you are quite outstanding, aren't they?'

'Are they?' Warrender looked amused. 'They are extremely readable. But it's hard for one to say what one was like twenty years ago. Certainly he is almost uncannily accurate about the terms I used then—I'd almost forgotten some of them—and about the ambitions of those early years. It seemed to bring a lot of things back to me, so I suppose he got it right. Though how a young man of his age could have done so I really don't know.'

She was tempted to tell him then of what Van had said about the inspiration of that school visit long ago. But it was, she reminded herself, for him to have the pleasure of explaining, if he wished so to do. When she joined Van the next evening at the studios, however, she told him what Sir Oscar had said.

'Yes——' he smiled with unconcealed pleasure— 'he phoned me and said he was very pleased. That I was to go on in the same vein, but to remember that he had his faults too. That rather amused me, because I hadn't glossed over his arrogance or his youthful conceit. But perhaps he doesn't think those rank as faults,' he added with a laugh.

Then he turned to the piano, propped up her score of *I Pagliacci* and began to play.

He was, as Miss Caterham had said, an accomplished and sensitive accompanist, and Kate found herself wishing that *he* had been chosen to play at the Gala Concert. He made few comments, allowing her to take the lead, in the knowledge that she was carrying out—or thought she was carrying out—Sir Oscar's instructions. At the end he said,

'I see why Warrender was impressed. You'll make a good Nedda one of these days if you go on working hard. In fact——' he laughed—'Francesca Poli will have to look to her laurels!'

'Who will?' Something plucked uneasily at the strings of Kate's memory.

'Francesca Poli. She's one of the best Neddas today. As a matter of fact, she's going to sing the Silvio–Nedda duet with your friend Carlo Ertlinger at some big charity Gala near the end of the month.'

There was a slight pause, then Kate said in a small voice, 'She isn't, you know.—I am.'

'*You* are?' He turned and stared at her. 'But Ertlinger—whether one likes him or not—is a top-liner, while you, if I may say so, are just a beginner, professionally speaking.'

'You may say so,' she assured him. 'It's true. No one knows it better than I do.'

'Well then, how did it come about? Did *Warrender* make the choice of substitution?'

'Not exactly,' Kate said. And then she tried to explain how it had all come about, but she felt she was making rather a poor job of it. At any rate, Van's expression grew less and less congratulatory, and at the end he said grimly,

'Then in a sense you're Ertlinger's protégée rather than Sir Oscar's.'

'No, I'm not,' she retorted defensively, and she firmly dismissed from her mind what Carlo had said about his plans for them to do quite a lot of things together. 'It's just that the other one—

Francesca Poli—cancelled and Carlo was in a spot. He happened to come in while Sir Oscar was auditioning me and—and one thing just led to another,' she finished lamely.

'I see,' said Van. And she realised he did not much like what he saw.

'You mean you don't approve?' She was nervous and sounded slightly angry, which was the last thing she wanted to sound.

'It isn't my business to approve or disapprove, is it?' he said, and although the words were reasonable enough, the tone was a good deal less friendly than it had been recently. 'I wish I were playing for you, that's all.'

'Oh, I *wish* you were,' she cried, with such emphasis that he smiled slightly and asked, as a matter of interest, who was accompanying her and Carlo.

'I don't know.' Kate shook her head. But as they left the studio together he said, 'I'll find out.' And she decided she also would make some enquiries on her own account.

Consequently, the next day she asked Sir Oscar if he knew who was playing for the Gala Concert.

'There'll be more than one accompanist,' he informed her. 'It would be a mammoth task for anyone to undertake the lot. Incidentally, there've been two or three adjustments to the programme, apart from the one which involves you. Artists do tend to engage themselves generously for these affairs and then find that professional engagements require them to be elsewhere.'

'Do you know who will be accompanying Carlo and me?' Kate asked rather timidly.

Warrender reached for the post, which she had opened and set before him and said, 'I shall.'

'*You* will?' Fright and gratification overwhelmed her.

'Anthea is singing a couple of items,' he explained. 'They had a major disappointment and she agreed to take over. I shall be accompanying her, of course, and might as well accompany you and Ertlinger as well.'

'How—how good of you,' she stammered.

'Not at all. I prefer to have you in my hands on such an occasion,' he told her. 'So you'd better do your best. I shan't be available for anything but the actual performance. Someone else will have to do the dress rehearsal.'

'Oh, could Van Merton do it?' she exclaimed, suddenly pink with excitement.

'Is he good?' Warrender asked, as if he really wanted her opinion.

'Yes, he is,' she stated confidently. 'Miss Caterham told me he was very accomplished and very sensitive, and that's how I found him when he played for me.'

'Oh, Isobel Caterham answered for him, did she? Well, I'll see what Anthea says.'

Anthea said she would be happy to have Van Merton for the dress rehearsal if he were free, and so it was arranged. To Kate the fact that both Van and her famous uncle would, so to speak, have a hand in her dramatic debut added the most extraordinary attraction to the whole occasion.

'I'd have thought you would be nervous with Warrender checking every note,' Carlo said half scornfully. 'I'm not sure that he would have been my choice. Only of course one doesn't actually *refuse* Oscar Warrender's services. Who is this Van Merton, by the way?'

'He's the man who's writing that talked-of book about conductors,' Kate said casually. 'You met him once passingly when he was leaving the flat and you were just arriving. He's played for me once or twice for practice sessions. He's very good.'

'Well, if you feel comfortable about him, he'll do all right for me,' Carlo said with careless good humour. 'It's only the dress rehearsal, after all.'

In fact it was literally only at the dress rehearsal that the three of them finally came together. In a sense Kate was almost glad of this, as she felt nervous about the meeting between the two men. But her common sense told her that Carlo was being irresponsible in not ensuring that he met his unknown accompanist at least once before the important rehearsal.

'It's all right,' he assured her. 'I know the thing backwards and, provided *he* knows his job, neither of us need worry.'

'Typical,' was Warrender's comment when he heard. 'The eternal improviser. It gives a certain spontaneous charm to what he does, of course, but sets traps for the unwary. So long as it doesn't make you nervous——'

'I'm nearly dead with nervousness at the whole prospect,' Kate told him. 'But I feel better when I think of Van's support at the dress rehearsal, and your support on the night.'

'It would be absurd to admonish you not to be

nervous,' Warrender said realistically. 'Though, if it's any consolation to you, it will be Ertlinger they will have come to hear. Still, the British public are sentimental on the whole, and they like anyone who steps into the breach at the last moment. In addition, you are young and pretty. So unless you do something disastrous, which is unlikely, they'll be on your side. Anyway, I'll be there to uphold you on the night. You'll be all right.'

Strangely enough, Kate felt she would be. She even felt this to a certain degree when she arrived for the dress rehearsal, and was intrigued by the thought that Van Merton would at last be hearing how well she sang when Carlo was providing that extra *frisson* of excitement and feeling which was such an individual part of anything he did.

Their turn came fairly late in the programme, so that Kate had an opportunity to measure her own gifts against those of some of the other singers. Without undue complacency she felt she was not fatally outclassed, though with the star performers like Anthea, she did not even try to seek comparison.

Van obviously enjoyed accompanying Anthea, and acquitted himself well. In fact, Carlo, who was sitting with Kate in the half empty auditorium, said, 'Is that our chap? He's good.'

'Yes,' agreed Kate eagerly, and her spirits rose. But just then they received the signal to be ready in their turn and, with her legs feeling rather hollow, she went on to the platform with Carlo.

For a dreadful moment she wondered why on earth she had agreed to do this thing. It was like being in some terrible dream. Then Van smiled at her encouragingly, and the world swung into focus once more. The next thing she knew was that Carlo was singing. And, unbelievably, so was she.

Once more he wove that extraordinary spell. Once more she was responding. She was unaware that one or two people came into the wings and peered interestedly at her. Still less did she know that a quite important impresario asked, 'Who's the girl? She's good.'

What she was dazedly aware of was that there was quite an outbreak of applause from some of the other performers as Carlo and she went from the platform and that, from snatches of talk which she heard, it was not all for him.

'The best you've ever done!' he told her exultantly, his hand tight round her arm. 'Come in here for a moment and let me tell you just how good you were.' And he ushered her into his private dressing-room.

'You were wonderful, darling!' He uninhibitedly threw his arms round her and kissed her several times.

'But you were simply marvellous too,' she exclaimed. 'I sing so much better when I'm with you.'

'And you know why, don't you?' He looked down at her with smiling eyes. 'Because you and I were made for each other. Do you know that? This is only the beginning, Kate. It's fate, just as I told you. I can see us touring the concert world together—oh, don't laugh! It's true. It's something I've always planned to do, only the right girl was never there. Kiss me, darling, and say you agree.'

'But it's only the first time——'

'Kiss me,' he commanded.

So, half dizzy with excitement, she put her arms round his neck and kissed him more than once.

Neither of them heard the knock. Neither of them noticed the door open. Only, as Kate looked over Carlo's shoulder, she was suddenly aware that Van Merton was standing in the doorway.

CHAPTER SIX

As Van Merton withdrew, closing the door behind him, Carlo looked round and said, 'Who was that?'

'I don't know.' In something like panic Kate instinctively repudiated the very idea of Van's presence—and then hated herself for what she felt was a sort of disloyalty.

'It doesn't matter.' Carlo laughed easily. 'Whoever it was would realise he was unwelcome.'

'I suppose so.' There was nothing cheering in that thought, and she added immediately, 'I must go now. I have to ask——'

'No hurry,' he assured her. 'We've done our part in the proceedings and, as I was saying, we have quite a lot to discuss about our future.'

'No,' Kate told him resolutely. 'This isn't the moment to talk of the future in any serious terms at all. Be realistic, Carlo! This is the first time I've even *rehearsed* for an important professional appearance. I'm glad you're pleased and I hope everything will go well tomorrow. But as for the future—that's something else again, and not to be talked of just now.'

'Dear Kate! Always so serious, aren't you?' He laughed a little crossly, but he let her go. Though when he came with her to the door he would have kissed her again if she had not adroitly avoided him.

Not knowing quite what she proposed to say, she went in search of Van. But almost immediately she ran into Anthea, who told her that he had already left the theatre.

'He said he had an appointment elsewhere, but would see us both tomorrow. Incidentally, I found him an excellent accompanist and I'm sure you did too. You were awfully good, Kate, and Sir Oscar is going to be pleased with you tomorrow if you sing like that.'

'I hope so.' Kate smiled, but could hardly hide her frustration at not seeing Van without delay. She might then have been able to refer lightly to the incident in Carlo's dressing-room and reduce it to unimportance. As it was——

'Would you like Sir Oscar and me to pick you up tomorrow evening on the way to the theatre?' Anthea suggested at that moment. 'It would ensure your being there in good time and without fuss.'

'Thank you, I'd be very glad indeed,' Kate assured her, for she realised that what Anthea really meant was that it would give her a certain distinction to arrive in the company of the Warrenders.

Naturally Kate had been given a free day from office duties before the concert, so that she was rested and as calm as the circumstances permitted when the Warrender car arrived outside her modest flat the following evening. Sir Oscar was driving and Anthea sitting beside him in front. But as Kate got in at the back, her uncle turned to her and said,

'Anthea tells me you and Ertlinger put on a very good show at the dress rehearsal. I'll expect you to do as well—or perhaps a little better—tonight.' But he smiled at her kindly and she told herself again that his support was going to mean a lot to her.

The general atmosphere backstage at the theatre was a good deal more electric than on the previous day, and Kate became aware that she was moving up to a stiff test. A dress rehearsal—even one which went well—was one thing. An actual performance before a critical audience was quite another, and she felt her nerves tighten.

She was sharing the dressing-room with one or two other minor performers, and she was glad when someone said in a friendly way, 'That's a lovely dress you're wearing, and just right for you. It's a real blonde's green.'

'That's what my mother said when she bought it for me,' replied Kate rather shyly. And suddenly she thought very warmly of her mother and how proud she would have been to know that her daughter was making a sort of debut in the green dress.

'I'll phone her at the weekend,' Kate promised herself remorsefully, for she had not shared any of the recent hopes and thrills with her mother, mostly because she did not want to raise expectations which might come to virtually nothing.

Some of her fellow singers in the dressing-room made their contributions in the earlier part of the programme and all, on their return from the stage, reported that it was a 'warm' house and that everything was going well.

'It says on the programme that *Warrender* is accompanying you,' one of the girls said curiously. 'Is that a misprint?'

'No.' Kate smiled as casually as she could. 'I'm doing some secretarial work for him while his permanent secretary is in hospital. As he was going to accompany Lady Warrender tonight, he was kind enough to say he would accompany me—or rather, us—too.'

'Singing with Carlo Ertlinger and accompanied by Oscar Warrender! Not bad,' commented a bright-eyed young mezzo in a not entirely friendly tone. 'How did you do it?'

'I'm not sure myself,' Kate confessed so candidly that the others laughed goodhumouredly. And at that moment she received her summons to be ready in ten minutes' time.

Carlo was waiting for her in the wings, and took her hand in a warm, firm clasp, as he said, 'You look lovely, Kate. Don't worry about a thing. I'll look after you.'

Certainly she was glad of his presence as he handed her on to the stage to prolonged applause. But when the first chords sounded on the piano it was to Sir Oscar that she looked, and she was unspeakably glad to find that the piano was so placed that she could see him almost without turning her head.

It was true that she again took her emotional guidance from Carlo's beautiful, expressive tones. But the awareness of Oscar Warrender's commanding presence steadied her nerves unbelievably

and gave her a sense of such security that she felt a
sensation of pure joy surging through her.

'I've never sung like this before,' she thought
with one part of her awareness, but with the other
part of her she was simply Nedda singing in an
impassioned way with Silvio. It was the first time
she had found the real fusion between her intelli-
gence and her emotions, and the experience was
intoxicating.

At the end, as Carlo led her forward to receive
the plaudits of an enthusiastically delighted audience, she thought incredulously, 'I *enjoyed* it! It was
wonderful.' And her frank joy was so patent that
they applauded again.

Someone handed her a couple of bouquets as
she made her last appearance on the stage, with
Carlo standing back smiling and allowing her what
amounted to a solo call. Then he led her from the
stage, and Warrender who was waiting for them in
the wings said, 'Not at all bad for a first attempt.
We might make something really good of you one
of these days.'

Back in the dressing-room, she stood almost
dazed, looking at the flowers in her arms. Then
she examined the accompanying cards, and saw
that one bouquet was from the organisers of the
occasion, and the other was from Van. Cream and
pink roses, with the rather chillingly formal message on the card: 'Best wishes and good luck.
V.M.'

Afterwards there was a big party at one of the
leading hotels, where members of the public (for a
handsome sum which helped to swell the charity

receipts) were able to rub shoulders with the artists of the evening. Carlo kept Kate with him a good part of the time, so that she shared to a certain extent in the admiration showered on him by his admirers. But even when she was without his company several people came up to her, congratulated her and even asked for her autograph.

To her surprise—and even to her slight discomfort—a lively journalist cornered her and asked what it was like to spring into fame in a night.

'Oh, please! I haven't done anything of the kind,' she protested. 'I'm glad everything went well, and of course it was wonderful singing with Mr Ertlinger for the first time, but——'

'The first time?' He scribbled something down. 'That's interesting. You were standing in for Francesca Poli, weren't you?'

'It was a last-minute replacement. Otherwise there wouldn't have been much chance of my being chosen,' Kate assured him.

'Then it was also the first time you had Warrender for your accompanist, I take it?—Now what did *that* feel like, Miss Grayson? Most singers find him pretty formidable, I believe.'

'He was tremendously helpful and very kind,' Kate insisted. And then, to her immense relief, someone else actually tugged at her arm and, turning round, she found herself looking down at a small, elderly lady who seemed vaguely familiar to her.

'I simply must have a word with you,' she told Kate excitedly. 'I'm Susan Chantry—Mrs Susan Chantry. I know your mother quite well, dear, and she asked me to be sure to contact you while I was in London. I did meet you once or twice back home, but you wouldn't necessarily remember me. Of course I didn't know you as Kate Grayson then. That's your stage name, I take it. I knew you as——'

'I think I do remember you,' Kate interrupted, raising her voice to drown the disclosure of the name by which Mrs Susan Chantry most unfortunately remembered her. And then she went on in a much louder tone than she usually employed, 'How nice to see you. How long are you in London, Mrs. Chantry?'

There was despair in Kate's heart, but an almost sickening sense of relief flooded over her as Mrs Chantry said regretfully, 'I'm leaving early tomorrow morning, unfortunately. To Paris for a day and then on to Vienna. But I'm so glad I had a word with you. I'll let your dear mother know. She'll be *so* pleased that we got together. And you were lovely tonight, dear. So was that good-looking young man singing with you—I forget his name. And who was the accompanist? Such an impressive-looking man. What one means by *masterful*, I couldn't help thinking. I left my programme in the cloakroom, so I haven't got all the names clear, but I'll have time to check up on them all in the plane tomorrow. Now I mustn't keep you, because other people will want to talk to you. But I just had to say hello and good luck.'

Kate, feeling almost giddy after the ups and downs of horror and relief during this breathless speech, summoned a friendly smile and a few polite words, with which to waft Mrs Chantry on her way to Paris and Vienna. Then, taking evasive action as she saw the persistent journalist making for her once more, she firmly attached herself to Anthea, who said, 'Do you want to stay on, Kate? Oscar and I were thinking of going soon.'

'I'd be very glad to go too,' Kate declared. 'But——' she looked round distressedly—'I haven't seen Van yet, have you? I'd like to thank him for his flowers and—and say a word to him.'

'Didn't he seek you out? I'd have thought he would,' Anthea said candidly. 'He's over there with Oscar. We'll go and join them, shall we?'

So they crossed the room to where Van Merton was in animated conversation with Warrender. Both men turned as they came up and Kate said a little breathlessly, 'Thank you, Van, for the lovely roses. I was truly happy you sent them.'

'I'm glad you liked them. You were splendid, Kate.' He spoke quite pleasantly, but suddenly she knew that a certain distance had been set between them.

'And, Van,' she persisted, 'I want to thank you also for all your help during the last weeks, and above all for your playing for me yesterday. I wanted to thank you then, but—but I missed you.'

'That's all right,' he assured her coolly. 'You were otherwise engaged, I expect.'

She blushed scarlet, and turned away, to find her uncle's speculative glance upon her. So she said impulsively, 'Lady Warrender says you're just going and that you would kindly give me a lift.'

'Can you wait another half-hour?' Warrender

glanced towards the door. 'I see Trenton Waring has just come in and I want a word with him.'

'Yes, of course I can wait,' she said in a small voice.

'If you want to leave now,' Van told her, 'I'm just going, and I have my car here.'

She flinched really at the thought of a tête-à-tête with him at this point, but felt instinctively that she must not refuse even so small an olive branch— if indeed that was what it was.

'If I'm not dragging you away——' she began.

'No, you're not dragging me away. But here is someone coming who may claim a prior right to take you home,' he added drily, as Carlo made his way towards them.

'I'd rather——' she began, and even had her hand on Van's arm when Carlo came up with them and said, 'Kate, I have someone over here who wants to meet you.'

'I was just about to take Miss Grayson home,' Van said coolly.

'*I'm* going to take you home, Kate.' Carlo's handsome face flushed suddenly and he looked petulant. 'Come over here first. It's my agent Jim Blanchard who wants to meet you. He won't keep you long. And then I'll see you safely home. I'm sure Mr—Merton will understand.'

'Of course.' Van bowed distantly. 'Goodnight, Kate. Let me know if there's any more accompanying to be done.'

She had no choice then but to bid him goodnight and go with Carlo. But it was with a conscious effort that she produced a friendly smile for Jim

Blanchard—a heavily built man, with a pleasant expression and extremely alert dark eyes.

'I wanted to meet the heroine of the evening,' he said as he shook hands with her.

'I'm not anything like that,' she replied almost crossly. 'I was a minor performer in an evening where there were at least three first-rate stars.'

'But the first-rate stars were already familiar to most of the audience, Miss Kate,' he assured her. 'You may not have shone so dazzlingly, but you were a new light twinkling in the operatic firmament. That always makes for special interest. In any case, you're over-modest about your attainments. Two of the most knowledgeable critics asked me who you were. They were not going to give you headlines, I imagine, but they were definitely interested.'

'*Were* they?' she smiled tentatively now, her attention completely caught.

'Yes. Straws in the wind, of course.' His answering smile was frankly appreciative. 'But the right kind of straws, Miss Kate. Incidentally, Carlo has been telling me there's a possibility of your doing something together. Perhaps a short exploratory concert tour early next year.'

'But surely you don't think I'm ready for that?' She looked both startled and excited.

'We wouldn't aim at the leading cities at first, of course. But there are plenty of second-line places of interest who would welcome Carlo Ertlinger teamed with an attractive virtually unknown young soprano. How would that interest you?'

'Tremendously, of course!' she said breathlessly.

'But—why me? I mean, surely Carlo on his own could take his pick of first-line places. Why add a beginner—even a promising beginner, since you're kind enough to put it that way—to make it a somewhat lesser event?'

'A very sensible question,' Jim Blanchard conceded with a laugh. 'And the answer is——' he raised a large but authoritative hand to check whatever interruption Carlo was trying to make at this point—'the answer is that, so far as concert work is concerned, Carlo would himself be treading new ground. He's been exclusively an operatic singer up till now. Concert work is quite a different matter. What we're suggesting—almost on the spur of the moment, I might say—would be a try-out for him too, and would best be attempted in the second-line places suitable to your own present state of development.—All right, Carlo, what is it that you're dying to say?'

'Simply that this is not a spur-of-the-moment suggestion so far as I'm concerned. It's something I've thought about a great deal, only the ideal partner has never been forthcoming. Kate is just what I've been looking for. She's a gift from heaven.'

'I don't quite recognise myself in that guise!' Kate said with an incredulous little laugh. 'And I simply don't know what to say.'

'Of course you don't.' Jim Blanchard's tone was almost soothing. 'It isn't the sort of suggestion requiring an immediate decision. Just think it over. You might even discuss it with Sir Oscar, if you're on those terms. His advice would be valuable.'

'He'll say "no",' protested Carlo discontentedly.

'He loves saying "no". It makes him feel like God.'

Kate started an indignant denial of that, but Jim Blanchard laughed goodhumouredly and observed that if Warrender gave an unequivocal "no" to a professional matter it would be a brave—or a foolish—person who would undertake to contradict him.

'We'll leave it at that for the moment,' he decreed firmly. 'Let's see what's said of you in the reviews tomorrow—if anything. And now Carlo had better take you home. You must have had a tiring and exciting evening all told.'

So Carlo took her home and—perhaps realising this was not the moment to bombard her with argument or persuasion—he was sympathetically restrained. Only, when he bade her goodnight, he kissed her as though he had some right to do so and said, 'Don't turn down something that could mean so much to both of us, will you, darling?'

'I'll think it over very carefully indeed,' she promised him. 'And thank you, Carlo, for paying me such a compliment. When I think what an artist you are yourself I'm overwhelmed that you should consider me worthy to partner you in any way at all.'

That seemed to satisfy him, for he was smiling in a very contented way as he drove off.

Alone in her flat, Kate reviewed the events of the evening, and found some of them hard to believe even now. She could not help knowing that she had sung better than ever in her life before, and surely what she had done once she could do

again—given the right circumstances. The one
cloud on the evening was that she had still not
managed to put things right between her and Van.

But, transcending in importance both the triumph and the disappointment, was the extraordinary proposition from Jim Blanchard. Exciting
beyond measure of course, but in some odd way
disquieting.

'It's so *improbable*,' she told herself as she got
ready for bed. 'That's it! Things just don't happen
that way to virtual beginners, however well trained.
At least, I don't think they do.'

Then suddenly she was overwhelmed by physical
and mental exhaustion and wanted nothing more
than to sleep. But as sleep descended upon her like
a heavy curtain her last thought was, 'Everything
depends on the reviews in the morning.'

The reviews in the morning proved to be extremely satisfactory. Those which mentioned her
at all, that was to say. Two ignored her altogether,
one merely included her between commas among
those who had performed. But the two leading
reviewers picked her out as a most promising newcomer, and one even declared that she contributed
some of the best singing of the evening, adding that
since Oscar Warrender himself had accompanied
her, might one conclude that she was an exciting
discovery of his?

She hoped her employer would not be irritated
by this form of speculation. But when she presented
herself rather nervously at the office she found him
amused and interested rather than annoyed. He
was in any case in an excellent humour, having

received a note from Miss Caterham to the effect that her doctor had pronounced her sufficiently recovered to return to work in a week's time, provided she took things easily at first.

'Which means that you and she can divide things between you for a while,' he told Kate, 'giving you time to pursue your studies and her time to get herself back into the routine. What are your professional plans, by the way? Having worked yourself up into good form you don't want to let yourself slip back.'

'I was going to ask your advice,' she said boldly, though she quailed slightly at the prospect of detailing Carlo's plans.

'Yes?' He fixed her with that rather intimidating glance. 'I suppose Ertlinger wants you to listen to some wild plan of his?'

'How did you know?' She stared at him.

'I didn't imagine he trotted you over to Blanchard to discuss the weather,' was the reply. 'What is the proposition, Kate?'

She told him then and, to her surprise, instead of immediately turning it down he gave it some thought.

'Risky,' he said after a minute or two. 'Particularly at this stage. But there's no denying it could be a big thing for you if it came off. It might do young Ertlinger some good as well,' he added reflectively. 'It would involve some hard and concentrated work, which is what he needs at this point. Have you ever built up any kind of concert repertoire?'

'I did some modest concert work back home,'

Kate explained, immensely relieved to find she was actually discussing the plan seriously with Sir Oscar. 'I don't think you would have regarded it as outstanding.'

'Probably not. What sort of things did you undertake? Almost exclusively in English, I take it?'

'No. Some *arie antiche* in Italian, and some French songs of the Romantic period. As for German lieder——'

'No, you're not ready for that,' he interrupted and, dropping suddenly into Italian, he asked her some questions and listened attentively to her replies.

'Your accent is good,' he said. 'I noticed that in the Nedda.' Then he reached for the telephone, dialled a number and, to her mingled astonishment and disquiet, she heard him say, 'Is that you, Merton? I want you to do something for me. I'd like to send Kate along to you at the studios in the next few days. Take her through half a dozen songs of her own choosing—English and Italian and possibly a couple of French. Then have her sing them for me when she's ready. I want to hear what she does with them.—You can't manage anything before Friday?—That's all right. There's no overwhelming hurry. Thank you. She'll meet you at the studios at three-thirty on Friday.'

Kate noticed that he did not bother to consult her about *her* convenience before he replaced the receiver. But then no doubt he presumed—and correctly so—that she would know how to put first things first.

'Merton will handle that for you,' Warrender informed her, 'and I'll hear you some time next week. Don't make any euphoric plans until after that.'

'Oh, I won't! and thank you so much, Sir Oscar. You are *good*,' she exclaimed gratefully.

'Few people would agree with you there, I'm afraid,' he replied drily. 'But waste of good vocal material is something I cannot stand. I'll have to know just how far we can stretch you before I let you even consider this idea of Carlo's.'

Then he went off to a rehearsal, leaving her so little work that presently she plucked up her courage and telephoned Van on her own account.

He answered so curtly that she said timidly, 'Do I disturb you, Van? It's Kate speaking.'

'No, not at all,' he assured her. 'I was working, but I've reached a mental blockage and am glad of some distraction. This is a very interesting suggestion of Warrender's. Was it your idea that we should work together?'

'No,' she admitted. 'But I was delighted when Sir Oscar suggested it.'

'What's the idea behind it, Kate?'

She hesitated, reluctant to introduce Carlo's name and, in any case, feeling pretty sure that the plan must remain confidential for the time being.

'It's all very vague at the moment,' she said with truth. 'Sir Oscar thinks I just might be ready for some concert work in the not too distant future.'

'Do you mean *recital* work?—on your own?' He sounded astonished. 'That's a very specialised field,

Kate. I shouldn't have thought——'

'I know—I know,' she interrupted hastily. 'It's just an idea. There's absolutely nothing decided. Sir Oscar may reject me entirely when he hears me.'

'Not if I can help it!' declared Van, and suddenly she had the impression they were friends again. 'If there's a single thing I can do to help you impress Warrender as a born recitalist, I'm your man.' He laughed, and there was a note of challenge and excitement in the laugh.

'Oh, thank you, Van!' Kate wondered if her voice sounded as lilting to him as it did to her. 'I'm so grateful.'

'I'm only sorry we can't start before Friday. But the fact is that my sister is coming——' he stopped, as though he wondered why he had said that, and she asked tentatively,

'Is that the sister who—who has no reason to like my mother?'

'The very same,' he agreed regretfully. 'But don't worry, Kate. Even if you meet—which I hope you will—she won't know you under your present name. There's no need to feel awkward about—the past. I *want* you to meet her. I'm very fond of her and I think you and she would hit it off together.'

'Then I too should like us to meet,' said Kate, recognising this as an olive branch of truly handsome proportions; and on impulse she added, 'Van, talking of awkward moments—which we weren't actually, but very nearly so—there's something I want to explain. I felt a perfect fool when you saw Carlo embracing me in the dressing-room the other day. It must have looked like a Romeo-and-Juliet clinch, but it was really just an exuberant impulse on his part, following on an exciting success for us both. Please don't read anything else into it.'

There was a pause and then he said heavily, 'You mean you didn't want him to do it?'

His tone was so serious that, in her nervousness, she almost giggled, which imparted just the right touch of lightness to her voice as she replied,

'Look, Van, there isn't a girl alive who wouldn't like being kissed by a handsome, madly successful baritone. But the scene was certainly not of my seeking, and I wouldn't like you—or anyone else, come to that—to attach undue importance to it.'

'You relieve my mind,' he said, and she had not decided whether the tone was sarcastic or sincere before he added, 'See you at three-thirty on Friday, Kate.' And he rang off.

During that evening and the following day Kate felt happier than at any previous time during her stay in London. For one thing, her uncle was taking her seriously, professionally speaking; and for another, it seemed that a friendly footing had been re-established between her and Van. The thought of his sister and her unhappy part in Kate's own family life still disturbed her, but, she told herself, with her mother safely on the other side of the world, the situation should be perfectly manageable.

This reflection again reminded her a little guiltily that she owed her mother at least some account of the events of the past few weeks. So she settled down to write a long letter, emphasising her own modest hopes and playing down anything which might lead her volatile mother to entertain any exaggerated ideas.

Of Carlo she had heard nothing, and this surprised her, while it also in some way relieved her, for she had no wish to give substance to his plans until Sir Oscar had had time to give an informed opinion. Then in her newspaper the following morning she read a short item to the effect that Carlo had been flown to Paris to substitute for another baritone at a moment's notice, and would be away from the London scene for some days.

Kate naturally gave a good deal of time to re-examining the number of songs she had used in earlier days, and she was engaged on this pleasant task on the Thursday evening when she was called to the telephone. To her astonishment, the operator, having checked her identity, informed her that there was a call for her coming through from Australia.

'From *Australia*?' Kate tried to recall anyone she knew in Australia—particularly anyone who would actually telephone her from there. 'Yes, yes, of course I'll take it,' she added hastily as the operator repeated the query. Then, to her increasing astonishment, it was her mother's voice which sounded in her ear, so clearly that she might have been speaking on a local line.

'Mother! What on earth are you doing in Australia?'

'I'm on my way to London, darling,' cried her mother, in tones of such excitement and eagerness that she sounded like someone half her age. 'Susan Chantry phoned me from Paris a few days ago and told me about your great triumph. I can hardly believe it! And your uncle, who everyone says is such a *proud* man, actually *playing* for you, like any little accompanist! It's like a fairy story come true. Susan said the critics wrote that you sang better than anyone else that evening. And suddenly I thought—what was I doing on the other side of the world when all this was happening to my little girl? So I packed a few things then and there.— Yes, I know, I always *was* impulsive. But this is about the greatest moment of our lives. I'll be on my way again in about half an hour, and be with you in London, darling, in less than a couple of days!'

CHAPTER SEVEN

'MOTHER!' Kate felt as though she were in a descending lift that was out of control. 'Mother, it isn't a bit like that! Susan Chantry must have exaggerated wildly. It's true that my uncle accompanied me, but——'

'What's that, darling?—The line's not very good at this end.—Yes, I know your uncle accompanied you. That's the wonderful part. It shows what he thinks of you. And if *he* thinks you're wonderful everyone else will agree. Just as Susan said—the critics described your singing as the best in the evening, although there were several famous names on the programme. Oh, my dear, I can't *wait* to be with you and hear all about it. You sound so far away. So—so formal somehow.'

There was a sudden catch in her mother's voice, and then she said almost timidly, 'You are—pleased that I'm coming, aren't you?' And all at once Kate could visualise her, standing there with the receiver in her hand, dismayed by the idea that, inconceivably, the bottom might be about to drop out of what had been a dazzling world only a few minutes ago.

'I'm *delighted*!' Kate lied desperately. 'I'm simply overwhelmed with joy. That's why I sound stunned, I expect. Only, darling, don't build great castles in the air or you'll have a frightful disappointment.

140

All I had was a very nice success at a single concert.'

'But your uncle—the famous Oscar Warrender—actually played for you!' Obviously her mother simply could not move from that overwhelming fact. Equally obviously, it was going to be impossible in a few minutes—and at a distance of thousands of miles—to disabuse her of the notion that this in itself indicated the beginning of a successful career.

In any case, what could one do or say? It was too late to change the course of events—to insist that her mother returned to her New Zealand home. Even if that were possible, the mere suggestion would be a slap in the face of unimaginable cruelty.

So Kate said helplessly, 'It will be wonderful to see you, darling. When is your plane due in London?'

'I don't know,' replied her mother airily. 'It's always so difficult to work out times on the other side of the world, isn't it? I'll phone from the airport when I get in.—Oh, they're calling my flight number now and I must go! Goodbye, dear, goodbye. See you in London! I've never been more excited in my life.'

The line went dead and, having replaced the receiver, Kate buried her face in her hands.

Of *course* she would be happy to see her mother. Only not just now. Not when her whole life, and possibly her career, were in the melting pot. There were too many delicate complications to be considered. How, to begin with, was one to isolate a disagreably astonished Warrender from the sister-in-law he had no wish to meet?

Mother, with her naïve enthusiams and comments—Uncle Oscar, with his detestation of anything unprofessional in relation to the art which was his life. It was chalk and cheese, oil and water. Even Anthea would be dismayed at the entry of the excited amateur into the professional scene.

And then there was Van! She had forgotten about him until this moment; not to mention the unknown sister who was also due in London at any time now. How was she to deal with *that* problem? How, above all, was she to protect that new warmth which had begun to strengthen their friendship? She could see that new—and precious—intimacy dissolving before her eyes.

'There is just no way of explaining to *anyone*,' she told herself distractedly. 'I must somehow make Mother understand that, much though I love her, she's part of my life that I must keep separate from what's been happening to me here.'

There would be no way of making this decision palatable, and she winced at the thought of the pain and disappointment she would have to inflict. But the situation was not of her seeking. Indeed, she had gone to the utmost care to avoid just such a crisis. Now that it was upon them both she and her mother must do the best they could. Explanations might well be made at a later date. But just now, for a matter of weeks or possibly only days, her mother must be kept divided from her uncle and both Van and his sister.

By the time she met Van the following afternoon

at the studios her mind was completely made up. She found him in the most amicable and helpful mood. He approved her choice of songs, he expressed warm admiration for the way she sang them and—in a tactful and friendly way—made valuable suggestions for subtly improving the way she presented them.

'I can see why Warrender was anxious to hear you in this kind of thing,' he said. 'You sing these songs with a sort of intimate charm which makes a direct appeal to almost any type of audience. It's quite a rare gift. Many people tend to think that a simple song is simple to sing. Nothing could be farther from the truth. Any fool can warble them, of course. But to do them full justice requires innate artistry and hard work. I reckon Warrender is going to be pleased.'

'Oh, I do hope so!' She smiled with sheer pleasure at the thought, and forgot for a moment the complications which were creeping up on her private and professional life.

Then she remembered, and forced herself to ask casually, 'By the way, just when is your sister coming, Van?'

'On Sunday. That means we shall be able to do some more work tomorrow morning. But I'm afraid that on Sunday I shall have to keep myself free for her.'

'Why, naturally! Is she—is she coming from New Zealand?'

'From New Zealand? No, of course not. She lives in Edinburgh. Why should——? Oh, I see what you mean. You thought that because that awkward business happened in New Zealand she *lived* there. No, she was just on a visit at that time, Kate. It's all over anyway. Let's forget it, shall we?'

She nearly told him then and there about her mother's impending visit. But he was looking at her with such an air of friendly persuasion that she could not bring herself to say anything which might destroy the harmony of their present relationship. So she let the opportunity pass.

That evening she telephoned to one or two airlines in an attempt to discover when and from which direction her mother might be coming. But her own information was so scanty that she gave up the attempt and resigned herself to waiting until her mother should arrive and contact her.

It was late on the Saturday afternoon that the telephone rang and her mother's weary but unmistakable voice informed her that she was now at Heathrow and could dear Olga come and fetch her?

The use of her real name made Kate jump, and she realised that the first thing she had to do was to train her mother to call her Kate.

'It's Kate, darling,' she said, with as easy a laugh as she could manage. 'Don't forget! And I'm on my way this very minute.'

She called a cab and drove to the airport where, owing to one terminal being out of commission, there was a good deal of confusion. But she found her mother in the end, in the passenger lounge for European flights; and when she first caught sight of her—sitting beside her luggage looking very tired and forlorn—Kate felt a lump rise in her throat.

Her mother! However exasperating and illogical and unpredictable she might be, it was her mother—who had come halfway across the world because she loved her daughter and wanted to show her pride and delight in what she imagined to be her triumph.

'Mother——' Kate kept her voice gentle and quiet because she was half afraid of what the excitement of the meeting might do to anyone so tired and bewildered.

'Darling!' Her mother jumped to her feet, her face instantly radiant, flung her arms round Kate and burst into tears.

'Don't cry——' Kate kissed her several times. 'It's all right. I'm here, and I'm taking you straight back to my little flat, where you'll be at home and able to rest. You had some delay, didn't you? and you must be dead tired.'

'No, I'm all right now.' Her mother wiped her eyes and smiled brilliantly. 'It's just that I'm so excited and so happy. How lovely you look, dear. I'd forgotten you were so slender and a bit taller than me.'

'Oh, Mother, in a moment you'll be saying how I've grown!' declared Kate, and they both laughed and embraced again.

'Why, Kate!' She stiffened at the familiar voice behind her. 'What are you doing here? And who is this charming lady you are embracing? Introduce me, please.'

She turned slowly to face Carlo Ertlinger, handsome as ever and smiling with frank curiosity, and she realised there was nothing for it but to tell the truth.

'This is my mother,' she said simply.

'Your mother? I don't believe it. I thought perhaps—your elder sister.' And he took Lucy Warrender's hand and kissed it in a way that brought the colour to her cheeks and the sparkle to her eyes.

'I am Carlo Ertlinger, *signora*, and most happy to meet you. Where, may I ask, have you sprung from?'

'I haven't *sprung* from anywhere.' She gave him her really lovely smile. 'But I've flown, all the way from Australia, and from New Zealand before that. My daughter Ol——'

'Kate!' interposed the daughter hastily.

'Oh, yes, of course—Kate. Kate is going to be a singer, you see, and a very successful one, it seems. So I thought it was time I came to cheer her and encourage her.'

'And how right you are! No one knows better than I what a wonderful singer your daughter is. I sang with her at——'

'Of course you did! I remember the name now.'

'I'm glad to be remembered.' He was not, Kate saw, making snide fun of her. He was just enjoying the fact that he was charming her. 'As a matter of fact, Mrs Grayson——'

'My name is Mrs Warrender,' Kate's mother corrected him, and there was a stunned silence, which was broken by her adding, 'Oh, dear! I shouldn't have said that, should I?' She put her hand to her lips, like a child caught out in a fib.

'Well, it's certainly a name to conjure with,' Carlo agreed, with an air of enjoyment. 'Are you any connection of the famous Sir Oscar?'

She nodded and said, with a strange mixture of guilt and pride, 'I'm his sister-in-law.'

'Then Kate——' Carlo turned to the silent girl beside him—'you are Warrender's—er—niece?'

'Not quite,' she replied with a calmness which she found surprising herself. 'His brother, Professor Denis Warrender, was my mother's second husband. I was not his daughter. In fact, Sir Oscar usually refers to me as the so-called niece.'

'You mean he knows the connection?'

'Yes, of course,' Kate said coolly.

'And he doesn't acknowledge you openly?' Carlo sounded incredulous.

'Well, no. Why should he?' Kate laughed. 'If I want to make a career, I'd prefer to do it on my own name, not his.'

'If you were *my* niece—and of course I'm glad you're not—I should be so proud of you that I'd want to tell everyone,' he said with charming candour.

'Oh, Carlo, would you?' She could not help being touched. 'Well, people feel differently about these things, and you will do me a real favour if you keep this disclosure to yourself. I know I can rely on your tact and discretion.'

She was far from knowing anything of the sort, but he assured her that her family secret was now locked in his heart.

'May I drive you into town?' he suggested. 'I

have a car waiting for me, and it would give me great pleasure to take you.'

Kate's instinct was to refuse politely, but her mother exclaimed, 'How very kind of you! It would be a great relief. I really am tired now, and if it wouldn't be imposing——'

No imposition whatever was involved, it seemed. Nothing would please him better. . . . And in the shortest space of time a porter had conveyed his luggage and theirs to a waiting Daimler, and they were driving smoothly into town.

He sat in front, but turned from time to time to talk with them and presently he asked, 'Have you thought about Jim Blanchard's suggestion, Kate?'

'Yes, of course. But I haven't made any sort of decision yet.'

'Why not?' Kate was aware that her mother was listening with almost childlike interest.

'Well, I consulted Sir Oscar, and he wanted me to prepare a few songs for him to hear before any decision was made.'

'You mean he didn't turn down the suggestion out of hand? Come, that's something!' Carlo looked very satisfied, and then went on almost immediately, 'Have you started any sort of work on the project, and if so, with whom? Van Merton, I suppose. You know, it occurred to me——'

'*That* horrible man?' Kate jumped at the sound of her mother's violent objection. 'You don't want to have anything to do with him. He's a trouble-maker, if ever there was one.'

'Mother, *please*!'

'But it's true. You wouldn't know about it all,

but when I tell you he would have liked to have me in prison——'

'Don't say such things!' Kate exclaimed angrily. 'That's not true, anyway.'

'Perhaps,' said Carlo pacifically, though again his eyes were bright with interest, 'we're not speaking of the same person. Our Van Merton is a very fine accompanist, Mrs Warrender. Kate and I have both found him so. And if we should do a concert tour together,' he added carelessly, 'we might like to have him join us. In addition, I understand he is writing a book in which your distinguished brother-in-law appears. I don't think we can be talking of the same person.'

Kate feared that her mother would not be deflected so easily, but the magical reference to a shared concert tour took precedence over everything else.

'Do you mean——' she caught her breath on a gasp of incredulous excitement—'that you and Olga—Kate, I mean—are going to do a concert tour together?'

'It's a delightful possibility which we are exploring,' he assured her with a smile.

'But *you* are a very famous singer, aren't you?' She spoke with an air of artless admiration which even a tenor could not have resisted.

'And what makes you think your daughter isn't going to be a very famous singer too?' he countered teasingly.—'Oh, this is your place, isn't it, Kate?'

It was. And Kate had never been more glad to see it. Very cordial farewells were exchanged, and a few minutes later she was introducing her mother into her London home.

'It's small, of course,' she began, but her mother interrupted her.

'It's lovely, darling,' she said, hardly glancing round. 'But, Kate—you see, I can remember if I try—Kate, what a *darling* man! So kind and friendly, and not a bit conceited, although I believe he's world-famous, isn't he? I've remembered now why his name seemed familiar. I read an article about him when I was under the dryer at the hairdresser's. They said he was one of the leading baritones today.'

Kate agreed that this was so, and her mother hugged her almost ecstatically as she said, 'And he wants *you* to tour with him. Dear child, I can't think why you so persistently make so little of your terrific success. The most amazing things seem to have been happening to you. But,' she went on, before Kate could make another attempt to set the record right, 'there's one thing I *must* warn you about—that awful Van Merton. It *is* the same one, though I wasn't going to argue with that nice Carlo Ertlinger about it. Imagine the cheek of his presuming to write about your uncle. When I meet Oscar I shall tell him that——'

'Mother——' Kate spoke quietly but with great firmness—'there are quite a lot of things we have to get clear, and I don't want you to be hurt. But first of all—and most important—my relationship with Sir Oscar is in many ways quite a formal one. Basically speaking, I'm his secretary—and only a temporary secretary, come to that. I address him as "Sir Oscar" and he would be annoyed if I did anything else. In addition——'

'What a horribly conceited person he must be!' said her mother indignantly. 'Is she as bad?'

'Anthea Warrender is a darling,' stated Kate unequivocally. 'And in a way I'm fond of him too,' she added, rather to her own surprise. 'But he is a great man, Mother, with a tremendous position of authority. It's nothing to do with being conceited. World-famous conductors don't hobnob with just anyone.—Oh, dear, I'm not explaining this at all well!'

'Yes, you are, dear. You mean he doesn't want to meet me, don't you? Well, from what you've just said, I don't want to meet him either. I'm sorry for *her*, poor woman, but I suppose she's entirely under his thumb, and I wouldn't want to put her in an awkward position. I'm happy to have met your famous *unspoilt* Carlo Ertlinger, and I'm glad it was he who ran into us at the airport and not the Warrenders.'

This was not, of course, the impression of the Warrenders which Kate had wished to convey. But she realised that no amount of argument would alter her mother's opinion now. In any case, at least there would now be little difficulty in keeping her mother and the Warrenders apart. So she contented herself with saying,

'I haven't really given you the right idea of them, but I daresay if—I mean when—you meet them, you'll see for yourself how they are.'

After that she fussed affectionately over her mother, served her an appetising meal and, seeing that she was now drooping from jet-lag, she sent her to bed in her own bedroom. Later, as she herself went to bed on the divan in the sitting-room, she told herself that some of her worst anxieties had been dealt with fairly satisfactorily.

The next day was a pleasantly lazy affair, Mrs Warrender doing what she could to adjust to a totally different timetable. She was by nature resilient as well as optimistic, and Kate was moved to find how much she herself enjoyed having a companion again. She was not one to be bored by her own company, but she realised now that there had been a degree of loneliness in her life during the last many months. The life of a temporary secretary travelling round the world had presented many interesting features, of course. But passing contacts, however agreeable, had not entirely compensated for the lack of a day-to-day companion. Her mother now filled that want, and if her observations and opinions were not always along the same line as Kate's own, the genuine affection between them provided a happy common ground.

'I hope you won't be lonely while I'm away at the office all day,' Kate said a trifle anxiously as she was about to leave the flat the next morning. But her mother declared that, apart from still wanting to rest a good deal, she would greatly enjoy exploring on her own account and renewing her knowledge of the London she had known in her youth.

Reassured, Kate set off for the Warrenders' apartment, and when her employer asked her how she was getting on with her work on the songs, she told him at some length and with considerable enthusiasm what she had been doing.

Sir Oscar nodded with what seemed to be approval and said, 'Get Merton on the phone, will you? If he's available this afternoon ask him to come along. I have a couple of hours free then and I can't say just when I'll have time after that.'

'I have a lot still to do on most of those songs, you know,' Kate hastened to warn him.

'Of course. But I ought to be able to arrive at some sort of opinion. If you're no good we may as well face the fact now and abandon the idea. If there are possibilities we should involve Carlo at an early stage. Incidentally, have you any ideas about an accompanist? We should have his or her co-operation as soon as possible.'

'We—haven't discussed it yet.'

'No? Well, you could do worse than Merton himself—if he is willing and available, that is.'

'I thought that too,' said Kate, and, feeling suddenly excited, she reached for the telephone.

Fortunately Van was at home and immediately agreed to come along that afternoon.

'I have a fresh batch of material for the book,' he told Kate. 'I'll bring that with me and leave it with the Warrenders for consideration. You might tell him so.'

Kate passed on the message to her employer, who observed thoughtfully, 'That's a very gifted fellow. And he knows how to make one talent serve another. It's unusual to be so intensely musical and have a talent for writing as well. He should go far.'

She was surprised at the glow of personal satisfaction these words conveyed to her. She could scarcely remember now how greatly she had feared and resented Van's very presence at one time. Today it warmed her heart to hear him praised— still more to have it suggested that, if she and Carlo did enter on this exciting project, Oscar Warrender himself considered Van to be an excellent collaborator. It might be difficult, of course, to maintain complete harmony between the two men. But both had a keen awareness of what best served their professional interests, and this should surely weigh with them.

'I mustn't let my hopes run away with me,' she told herself. 'Sir Oscar may dismiss the whole idea once he's heard me.'

There was, however, no question of Sir Oscar's doing any such thing. He listened for some time without offering any comment. But Kate found this did not affect her inner confidence. She knew he was giving her his full attention, and she also felt the most wonderful support from Van. It was as though they were in some sense an indissoluble alliance, depending for understanding and expression upon each other.

'It's a remarkably good combination,' was what Warrender said when he finally spoke, as though he too were assessing them in conjunction with each other. 'Unusual for two people to be in such harmony. Let me call Anthea and hear what she has to say.'

So Anthea joined them in the studio and Warrender, without giving her his own views, merely said, 'Let's hear what you have to say about Kate in this type of programme.'

Anthea also listened with great attention and then said, 'I like your way of presenting songs, Kate, and your feeling for different styles is quite remarkable. Best of all I like the rapport between you two. It's as though you'd been working together for years. You know, you ought to try making a professional partnership of it.—Oscar, don't you think that if they worked hard together for six months or so they might be quite outstanding?'

'Yes, that's what I also think,' he agreed. 'At any rate, the possibility is there to such a degree that it would be foolish to ignore it.'

Kate turned to Van, who was still sitting at the piano, and her eyes were bright and there was a streak of excited colour in her cheeks.

'Van, what would you think of trying the idea? It's for you to say. You have so many other talents—so many other plans. The book, for instance——'

'Most of the work has been done on that by now.' He indicated the pile of manuscript he had brought with him. 'If you seriously thought of attempting a concert career, Kate, and wanted me as your accompanist, I would say "yes" without hesitation.'

He got up from the piano and came to take both her hands in his. And as he stood there looking down at her she had the strange conviction that never before in her life had she been so happy.

Anthea gave an indulgent smile, and Sir Oscar said, 'Well, provided Ertlinger agrees, it looks as though we've got our team.'

'Ertlinger?' Van turned violently from Kate and faced Sir Oscar. 'What on earth has *he* got to do with it?'

For once Oscar Warrender looked taken aback. 'Why, the whole idea was his. His or Jim Blanchard's. Didn't Kate explain that it was to be a joint tour?'

'No, she did not.' Kate could not have believed that Van's tone and expression could harden like that.

'I thought it was to be confidential until I'd proved myself,' she explained hastily. 'That's why I didn't tell anyone until Sir Oscar had given his opinion. I—I thought it was confidential,' she repeated nervously.

'It was not confidential from me if you proposed to involve me personally,' he retorted.

'No, I see that now. It was stupid of me. But things moved faster than I expected,' she said almost pleadingly.

'Well, they've come to a dead stop now,' he informed her. 'There's no question of my taking part if Ertlinger is the prime mover in the scheme. Do you really suppose I would trail round the country, tinkling on the piano, while you and he made up to each other on the platform, clasping hands and smirking for a delighted audience? No, thank you! If that's the idea you can find another accompanist.'

And, gathering up his music, he walked out of the room, and two seconds later they heard the front door bang.

'Oh, dear,' said Anthea helplessly.

'What's got into him?' exclaimed Kate in utter dismay. 'How could he speak like that? What's the matter with him?'

'He's jealous,' said her uncle, stating the obvious in a rather bored manner.

'*Jealous?* Of whom?—Of what? Because we would have the centre of the stage and he'd be only the accompanist, do you mean?'

'No, of course not. Don't be silly.' Her uncle spoke almost indulgently. 'He thinks he's in love with you—and maybe he is, for all I know. He also thinks that Carlo has designs upon you. If that's so it would hardly make for a harmonious trio, one must admit.'

'But why didn't he explain?' cried Kate. 'If he feels like that, I'll drop Carlo and his plans. At least, I mean——' she stopped and suddenly looked extremely startled.

'Well, what exactly do you mean?' enquired Warrender. 'The suggestion of a modest concert tour came from Carlo and his agent, if I understand it correctly. In those circumstances, *they* can drop *you*, but the reverse is not so easy.'

'Yes, I see—I see.' Kate passed her hands over her face as though brushing away confused thoughts. Then she suddenly said, 'Sir Oscar, how good am I on my own terms?'

'As a solo recitalist, you mean?'

She nodded.

'That's very different from starting as an assistant artist to an already famous singer.' Her uncle rubbed his chin reflectively. 'With the backing of someone like Ertlinger—not to mention Jim

Blanchard—you would find your path greatly smoothed, and the chance of quick success would be much nearer your grasp. As a solo recitalist struggling to find a footing you would have to be satisfied with quite a modest career at first. Even with a fine accompanist,' he added drily.

'But after that?' She looked at him eagerly. 'With devoted work and——'

'That's the key phrase, Kate. Devoted work—and luck. There's always an element of luck in these things. Given absolute dedication on your part, and an occasional smile from fortune, you might make a very fine career indeed. In fact——' he gave her his rare smile—'I'd put my money on you, I think.'

'You would?' She flushed with pleasure. 'Then in that case——'

'No—wait!' There was a note of stern authority in his voice. 'I suggest you go home and think very carefully over what has happened. At your age it's difficult to know with certainty what one really wants of life. To decide on impulse is unwise at any age.'

'Thank you,' said Kate, and she went slowly from the room, vaguely aware that Anthea made a move to go with her, but that a slight gesture of Warrender's expressive hand stopped her.

CHAPTER EIGHT

It was all very well for her uncle to advise her to 'go home and think it over,' reflected Kate. What he did not know was that Mother was at home, eager to hear anything in connection with her daughter's future, but unfortunately the last person with whom to discuss the present complicated situation.

She walked slowly into the Park and, as though by instinct, sat down on the seat where twice before she had reviewed a personal crisis—the first time when she had boldly gatecrashed into her famous uncle's life, if only as a humble secretary, and the second when she and Van had parted in such anger and come together again with such strange joy.

Today they had also parted in anger. But whether they would ever come together again was now complicated by so many other considerations that she felt more unsure and bewildered than ever before in her life.

Characteristically, Oscar Warrender had reduced the choice to its simplest terms. She could accept the remarkable offer made by Carlo and Jim Blanchard, providing herself with a probable short cut to artistic success but erecting an impassable barrier between herself and Van. Or, on the other hand, she could reject the best professional offer she was ever likely to receive and humbly ask

Van to join her in the long, hard struggle to make what Warrender had cautiously described as 'a modest career'.

'He thinks he's in love with you,' her uncle had said of Van almost carelessly, 'and maybe he is, for all I know.'

What was the good of his *thinking* he was in love with her? she asked herself angrily. Didn't he *know*?

And then, in a moment of cool self-analysis, she looked at the other side of the question. What, if it came to that, did she know about *her* feelings for *him*?

It is a fact that in most people's lives there are occasional breathtaking moments when truth strikes with the force and shock of a cold water jet. Just such a moment struck Kate then and she gasped—half frightened, half enthralled by the sudden finality of the experience. For *of course* she loved Van! though she could not have said by what degrees that state of feeling had come about. She loved him, and it was anguish to know that a jagged rent had been torn in the fabric of their relationship.

When her uncle had spoken of 'a modest career' her high hopes had received a slight check. But did it really matter how modest the career so long as she made it with Van? And if he loved her he would surely feel the same.

Only—suppose he did not really love her? Suppose he simply regarded her as a very agreeable partner—someone who would be of value as he made his own way up the professional ladder?—

What then? She would have thrown away the chance of a lifetime for something which could bring only pain and disillusionment.

It had to be one or the other—she saw that now. In fact, she must have been absurdly naïve to suppose she could make a career which involved them both. It was, quite simply, Carlo or Van.

She sat there for a few minutes longer, telling herself that she was taking time to make up her mind. But her mind was already made up, and what mattered most now was to speak to Van and assure him that she was abandoning all thought of that tour with Carlo.

It was vital to get home and telephone him as soon as possible. She went out of the Park, hailed a passing taxi, and was on her way home before she remembered once more that her mother would probably be there, to add a further complication. But she would have to deal with that as best she could. The important thing was to speak to Van before he had time to feel the whole question had been irrevocably settled.

To her well concealed irritation, she found her mother was indeed at home and, judging from her excited expression, it seemed she had had a very satisfactory day.

'What's been happening?' Kate smiled at her a trifle absently. 'You look pleased and excited, somehow.'

'Well, yes, I suppose I am.' Her mother laughed. '*Two* things happened this afternoon. One very nice, and one not so nice but rather useful.'

'You'd better tell me the nice one first.' Kate

spoke indulgently.

'Dear Carlo Ertlinger phoned and is going to take you and me out to dinner tonight. He said he would fetch us about seven. I did suggest that perhaps he would prefer to take you on your own (because I don't want to be the interfering mother, you know), but he said—no, certainly not, that he wanted to get to know me really well. I think that was nice, don't you?'

'Very nice,' agreed Kate, making a few hasty readjustments in her own mind, and wondering if she could, in the nicest way possible, take the opportunity of telling Carlo that she had made up her mind to refuse the concert tour. It might be easier with a third person there. Then, remembering there was more news to come, she asked what the not-so-nice item was.

'Well——' her mother's expression underwent the most extraordinary change, and she looked for a moment like an obstinate child who knew she had done something naughty but felt it was worthwhile. 'That objectionable Van Merton phoned——'

'Mother!' Kate stiffened with sudden apprehension. 'He wanted to speak to me, you mean? *When* did he ring?'

'Oh, about twenty minutes ago, I suppose. I know you won't be pleased, but I had to act on my own initiative. You see, you wouldn't let me tell you how terribly he behaved back home a few years ago, so it's difficult for you to understand why I had to act with great firmness. But, as your mother, I felt it was up to me to protect you from——'

'What are you talking about?' Kate was aghast.

'Don't look like that, dear. It's all over now. You will have no unpleasantness. I've dealt with him. He asked to speak to you and I said there was no question of it. Then he asked who I was and I said I was your mother——'

'You *told* him?'

'Certainly I told him. I wanted him to know I had the authority to speak on your behalf. And I *am* your mother, dear. I'm not ashamed of it—and I hope you aren't either.'

'Go on,' said Kate, closing her eyes for a moment.

'He said he was surprised to find I was here in England, and I told him that was no business of his. I added that I'd explained to you about his shocking behaviour towards me and that you had absolutely no intention of seeing him or speaking to him again.'

'You couldn't have said such a thing!' Kate was white and trembling with what she recognised as raging fury, and her mother put out a hand to calm her.

'Dear, you don't understand. His conduct was abominable. I'll tell you about it later when you're less excited, and you'll agree with me entirely.'

'I shall do nothing of the kind,' cried Kate. 'How *dared* you interfere like that?'

'Kate, don't speak to me in that tone! I'm your mother, and I acted for the best. What are you doing?'

'I'm telephoning to Van now, to apologise and tell him it's a ghastly mistake.' She seized the phone and dialled his number with a shaking hand, while her mother continued to repeat,

'I acted for the best. He's a horrible man. I couldn't let you go on being friends with him. You don't understand——'

Then a totally unknown female voice said, 'Hello. This is Van Merton's apartment.'

'Can I speak to him, please?' Kate wished her voice sounded less choked and strained.

'I'm afraid not. He's out. Would you like to leave a message?'

'No. Who is that speaking?'

'I'm his sister. If there's anything you would like me to tell him, he'll be in for a short while this evening.'

'Perhaps—I'll ring—tomorrow,' Kate said desperately.

'You won't find him at home then. We're leaving for Edinburgh early in the morning. If you like to leave a message——'

'No. No message,' Kate replied heavily. Then she replaced the receiver and there was a deep silence in the room. Finally, her mother spoke in that half timid tone Kate usually found so touching.

'I'm sorry if I did the wrong thing,' she said. 'But he made me suffer so much. He frightened me—threatened me. If Denis were here he would back me up in what I'm saying. Kate, he can't really mean anything to you.'

'No?' She sank into a chair and let her mother's voice wash over her, without paying much attention to the words. It was as though the decision had been made for her. Oh, there might be some possibility of trying to explain some time in the future. But how? and when? He was a proud man and a high-tempered one and—justifiably or not— he already thought she had been less than candid with him in relation to Carlo.

Presently she realised that her mother had put a cup of tea beside her, rather as one might seek to placate an angry dog, and she said, 'I'm so sorry, Olga—Kate, I mean—perhaps I shouldn't have come to London, after all.'

'It doesn't matter.' Kate absently drank the tea. 'Perhaps it was fate's way of making the decision for me.'

'What decision, dear?'

But Kate shook her head, unable to go into any explanations now. What was the good, anyway? Van had been given his marching orders, and he was in a mood to accept them, bitterly and finally. He would be leaving for Scotland in a matter of hours, and Carlo was left in possession of the field. Carlo—who was going to take them out that evening and set himself to charm her mother and talk persuasively of her own future.

In spite of some rather pathetic attempts at conversation on her mother's part, Kate could not bring herself to manage more than a few words in reply. But when her mother said tentatively, 'Would you rather not go out this evening, after all?' she drew a long sigh and replied,

'We might as well go. It would be hard to put off Carlo now.' And, although she did not say so aloud, she added to herself, 'What does it matter,

anyway? At least he'll make me think of other
things.'

To an unexpected degree, this was true. Carlo
took her and her mother to a charming restaurant—elegant, intimate, with perfect food and
wine, and service to match.

'It's lovely! I've never been in a nicer place.' Lucy
Warrender looked round with the frankest
pleasure, and their host laughed and declared that
she was the ideal person to entertain.

'You will come to hear me sing one night, won't
you?' He smiled at her in that compelling way. 'I'm
really quite good on the operatic stage. Kate will
vouch for me.'

'Yes, of course. There's nothing I should like
better,' Kate's mother declared. 'We'll get tickets
the very next time you are singing.'

'Pardon me, but *I* shall get tickets for you the
next time I sing,' he assured her. 'And when Kate
and I go on tour——'

'That hasn't been determined yet,' Kate interjected quickly.

'You mean Warrender refuses to make up his
mind?'

'No,' she said slowly, 'I don't mean that.' And
then she recognised this as the first moment of
decision. 'As a matter of fact, he was a good deal
impressed when he heard me. You'll have to talk it
over with him. But I—I myself haven't quite
decided yet.'

'But, darling, what is there to decide?' He looked
at her with shining eyes and almost consciously
brought the whole weight of his attraction to bear

upon her. 'If Warrender is for it, what possible objection can you have?'

'I want time. You can talk to Sir Oscar about it when you like, but——'

'You mean literally when I like?' He put his hand over hers as it lay on the table, and she nodded.

'Then I will do so now,' he said, getting to his feet. 'Warrender has just come into the restaurant with Anthea.'

'Oh——' said Kate helplessly.

And, 'Oh!' said her mother on a note of protest.

Carlo disregarded both exclamations, and went forward to greet the Warrenders and bring them to his table.

'Kate and I were just discussing——' he began, and then broke off to say, 'Of course you know this is your sister-in-law, don't you?'

'Lucretia!' exclaimed Anthea, while for half a moment of pregnant silence Warrender surveyed the now frightened small woman who had risen instinctively to her feet.

Than he held out his hand to her and said, 'So you are my brother's wife? He wrote to me more than once about you, telling me how happy you made him. I must thank you.'

'Oh——' the ready tears came into Lucy Warrender's eyes, but she blinked them back and smiled timidly. 'I—I didn't expect you to say any-thing like that to me.'

'No?' Sir Oscar gave her that rare and rather beautiful smile which he usually kept for Anthea. 'But it needed to be said, didn't it? This is my wife, who has been wanting to meet you for some time.'

Anthea uninhibitedly kissed Kate's mother and said, 'It's nice to meet you at last. But I'm afraid we're interrupting your meal.'

'That's all right,' Carlo put in quickly. 'In fact, I really wanted to speak to you, Sir Oscar, about persuading Kate to join me in a concert tour. She tells me that you approve in principle——'

'We will discuss it another time and in more suitable surroundings,' Oscar Warrender said, and his keen glance passed over the pale Kate, taking full note of the varied emotions from which she was suffering. Deeply moved by his reception of her mother, hopelessly irresolute about the decision Carlo wanted to force upon her, she was obviously distressed.

Turning to Carlo, he added with authority, 'Don't badger my niece about this tour tonight. We will talk of it later.' Then, with a comprehensive little nod which included all three of them, he took Anthea by the arm and ushered her to a distant table, and paid no more attention to them for the rest of the evening.

'He called me his niece for the first time—and in public,' Kate said wonderingly.

'I never expected him to be like that!' Lucy Warrender's tone was almost awed. 'You didn't *describe* him that way, Kate.'

'No.' Kate shook her head slightly. 'He isn't always like that.'

'He's very seldom like that,' corrected Carlo with a laugh. 'But, since the great man decrees it, we'll leave the subject of the tour for the moment.' He scrupulously kept his word about that, and Kate had the most extraordinary impression that, in calling her his niece, her uncle had for the first time thrown the mantle of his protection round her.

For the rest of the evening she forced herself to be as cheerful and responsive as she could, but she was glad when it was over and Carlo took them home. The determination had been growing within her that just once more she would make the attempt to speak to Van, but she would have to wait until her mother had gone to bed.

Fortunately, excited though she was about the events of the evening, Lucy Warrender was still suffering a certain degree of jet-lag. And half an hour after they had returned home Kate was sitting by the telephone, nervously dialling Van's number.

The bell at the other end rang for a long time, and she had almost abandoned hope when his voice said sleepily, 'Yes? Who is it?'

'Oh, Van! It's Kate,' she said eagerly. 'I have to speak to you—to explain——' And then she stopped dead, for quite distinctly she had heard the receiver at the other end firmly replaced, and he was a hundred—a thousand miles away.

Momentarily anger dried the tears on her cheeks, though nothing could assuage the sick dismay in her heart. It was over. The finality with which that receiver had been replaced told her that beyond question.

After a while she forced herself to believe with bitter resolution that she was lucky to have had the matter decided this way. Before it was too late she had been prevented from taking a fatal step, from involving herself with someone both cruel and unreasonable. She was lucky—she was lucky! For now she could accept Carlo's offer without thought of any alternative. With him she would make, not just a modest career, but perhaps a distinguished one. And on this happy thought she buried her face in her hands and wept.

The next morning Kate took herself off to Killigrew Mansions in a state of some nervousness. True, Oscar Warrender had accepted the unexpected appearance of the unwanted sister-in-law with some grace, but that might have been no more than a polite way of glossing over an awkward social occasion. As Kate's employer he would be justified in feeling irritated—if no more—at the way in which she had somehow mixed personal matters with professional ones.

'He'll look at me in that intimidating way of his,' she thought gloomily, 'and I shall stammer and sound guilty.'

But this was not at all what happened—at least at first. For one thing, Miss Caterham chose this day to make her reappearance and, in welcoming her warmly, Warrender overlooked any lesser matter. She declared herself ready to take up her duties immediately, but he would have none of that. During the next few weeks, he told her, she could look in from time to time. But, for the time being, she was to join Anthea over coffee and he and his temporary secretary would deal with anything requiring attention.

Reluctantly, Miss Caterham yielded and, as the door closed behind her, Warrender reached for a report he had been examining earlier and became immersed in it. Then, ten minutes later, without looking up, he asked, 'How long has your mother been in London, Kate?'

'Only a day or two,' replied Kate, in a placatory manner which he seemed to find foolish, because he observed drily,

'It's a free country. There's no reason why she shouldn't come if she wanted to. But what prompted the visit?'

'Well—it sounds silly, I know, but a casual acquaintance happened to be at the concert the other night and she telephoned a most exaggerated account of it to my mother. Mother got the idea that I was enjoying some extraordinary triumph and that she should be here to support me and—and share it.'

'What, exactly, made her draw such dramatic conclusions?'

'Mostly the fact that you accompanied me,' Kate told him apologetically. 'She's convinced that this in itself must constitute the beginning of a distinguished career.'

'Flattering—if inaccurate,' said Warrender. Then, abandoning the report and giving her his full attention, he asked curiously, 'Had she met Ertlinger before? You all seemed on very good terms.'

'Oh, we ran into him at the airport when I was there meeting Mother. I—I had to introduce her. And last night he kindly insisted on taking us out to dinner.'

'In very friendly circumstances?'

'Yes, of course.'

'Then, with regard to the projected concert tour, do I gather that friend Merton has irrevocably blotted his copybook?'

'It's more,' said Kate, with unexpected coolness, 'that *I* have irrevocably blotted *my* copybook'

'Oh?' He raised his eyebrows. 'Would you care to explain further?'

'No,' replied Kate. Then, suddenly overwhelmed by a wild desire to tell *someone*, she added, 'Yes.'

'Well,' said her uncle, 'which is it?'

'I think—I should like—to explain,' said Kate. 'If you don't mind listening.'

'I don't mind listening,' Warrender told her.

'I have to go back a long way.' Kate pushed back her hair with a nervous little gesture. 'Some years ago Mother somehow got herself involved in what nearly became a libel action——'

'I know about that.'

'Oh? Do you also know that it was Van's sister who was the person concerned?'

'No, that I didn't know.'

'Well, she was. And—and, according to my mother, Van made himself very unpleasant. She says he frightened and threatened her, but she may be exaggerating. At any rate, my stepfather—your brother—got her out of the trouble, but she's always remembered Van with fear and dislike. By the time she came here I'd already heard Van's version of the story and we'd——' she bit her lip at the recollection of this—'decided to put a line under the past. But of course Mother's arrival in London threatened all sorts of complications, particularly as Van's sister chose the same time to come from Edinburgh on a visit. Oh, dear, this is all very complicated, isn't it?'

'No, you're doing quite well,' her uncle said. 'You almost qualify for writing programme notes on boring new works. Go on.'

She laughed shakily and continued, 'I hadn't told Van about Mother's coming to London. I was waiting for the right moment.'

'The right moment seldom comes of its own accord, but it's difficult to decide when to grasp the nettle,' Sir Oscar conceded. 'So you mean that Van Merton was still unaware of your mother's presence in London when he stormed out of here yesterday, vowing to have nothing to do with the Ertlinger project?'

Kate nodded slowly, and her voice was not quite steady as she said, 'He telephoned before I got home, and Mother took the call. I suppose they were equally appalled and I'm afraid some dreadful things were said. Finally Mother, with the best of intentions——'

'But of course,' murmured Warrender.

'—informed him that I now knew all about his disgraceful behaviour and never wanted to see or hear of him again. She was honestly convinced that she was protecting me from someone she regarded as an arch-villain.'

'I'm sure she was,' said her uncle drily. 'But I hope you didn't leave it at that, Kate. I shall have a very poor opinion of you if you did.'

'Of course I didn't! I telephoned immediately to try to explain, but only his sister—whom I've never met—was at home. She asked me to leave a message. But I *couldn't*, you know. Not with a complete stranger, who probably thought me and my family pretty ghastly anyway. She said he would be in for only a short while that evening and that they were going to Edinburgh early the next morning. That's—today,' she added, more desolately than she knew.

'And you accepted that as final?' There was the slightest touch of contempt in Warrender's voice. The contempt of someone who invariably directed events instead of yielding to them.

'No.' She shook her head again. 'Last night, when Mother was in bed, I telephoned to Van again.' There was a long pause, which Warrender did not attempt to break. Then she cleared her throat and added, 'When I told him who I was he simply replaced the receiver without a word.'

'I trust,' said her uncle bracingly, 'that you were healthily furious at that point.'

'As a matter of fact I was,' replied Kate with some surprise. 'That was the moment when I decided I'd had enough of his high-handed ways and——' she raised her chin defiantly—'that I would accept Carlo Ertlinger's offer.'

'I see.'

'You mean you don't approve of my decision?'

'I mean that decisions taken in acute anger are often—though not invariably—regretted later. Will you accept a piece of advice from someone who is old enough to be—at least your uncle?'

'Ye-es,' said Kate uncertainly.

'Don't commit yourself for a day or two. This

is——' he glanced at the desk calendar—'Tuesday. If by Friday you are still of the same opinion, I will arrange for Ertlinger to meet us here on Saturday afternoon to discuss the outline of this concert tour.'

'You mean——' real animation and excitement flashed into Kate's face—'that *you* will advise and act for me in any discussion?'

'Oh, certainly. I am not allowing you to be exploited either by agents or ambitious colleagues. This is, after all——' he smiled grimly—'a family affair. And since it *is* a family affair, I think we should ask your mother to join us, don't you?'

'She'd love it!' Kate flushed because she was oddly moved. 'She would be so pleased and so— flattered.'

'Very well. I suggest you contrive not to see Carlo between now and then—and certainly not to discuss anything with him.'

'I promise,' Kate said earnestly. 'And—thank you.'

Absolutely no further reference was made to the discussion during the rest of the day, and when Kate went home in the evening all she said to her mother was, 'Sir Oscar may be having a talk with Carlo and me about the possible concert tour—on Saturday afternoon. He thought you might like to be there too.'

'*He* thought I might like to be there? Oscar, you mean?'

Kate nodded.

'Extraordinary man,' said Lucy Warrender. 'Denis always said he was unpredictable. But yes, of course I shall be delighted to come.'

Wednesday and Thursday passed very slowly, and yet Friday was all at once upon her with fearful suddenness—or so it seemed to Kate. But her resolution remained unchanged, and on Friday afternoon she told her uncle that she was determined to stand by her decision.

'Very well.' Warrender nodded almost carelessly. 'Anthea and I will expect you and your mother tomorrow afternoon at three o'clock.'

And the following afternoon at three o'clock, Anthea was warmly welcoming a pale but composed Kate and a flushed and excited Lucy Warrender. A few minutes later the conductor himself came into the room in what was, for him, an unusually genial mood.

'It's so kind of you to take such an interest in Kate's career,' Lucy Warrender said, with a sort of nervous eagerness. 'So difficult for *me* to advise her about anything to do with her profession, of course. But you know everything about it, don't you?'

'I wouldn't claim absolute infallibility,' replied her brother-in-law gravely. 'But on the subject of a concert tour I can offer some useful advice, I expect.'

'Oh, I don't doubt you can,' Lucy reassured him kindly. 'And it's fortunate Carlo Ertlinger is such a delightful person. So friendly and unspoilt. Kate will be very happy working with him, I'm certain.'

That was the moment when Kate, with inexcusable vacillation, doubted to the bottom of her heart that she would be anything but profoundly unhappy on this concert tour. She had an absurd, panic-stricken impulse to rush from the room, from the flat, from the situation which she herself had brought about. But it was too late, for she heard the front door bell ring. Carlo had arrived.

She turned to stare out of the window, and listened to his footsteps crossing the hall. She was aware that the door had opened, and she turned resolutely to face him.

Then she uttered an audible gasp, which was immediately echoed by her mother. For the man who had walked into the room was not Carlo Ertlinger. It was Van Merton.

CHAPTER NINE

'VAN!' exclaimed Kate softly and incredulously. 'Oh, Van, I thought you'd gone. I mean——' she added confusedly, 'I thought you were in Edinburgh.'

'I was,' he replied stiffly, but for some reason he seemed unable to take his eyes from her. 'Sir Oscar sent for me, saying it was urgent. I thought it was something to do with the book. But it seems——' he glanced round then and, for the first time, took in the presence of Kate's mother.

But before he could say any more Kate exclaimed, '*Sir Oscar* sent for you? But how——' she transferred her astonished gaze to Warrender —'how did you know where to find him? I thought it was—so hopeless.' And as the last word dropped into the silence it seemed to give the full measure of her own vain hopes.

'There are few addresses that Miss Caterham can't turn up when put to it,' replied her uncle casually. 'And Merton's literary agents were very helpful.'

It was at this point that Lucy Warrender found her voice and, in a tone which shook with mingled anger and fright, she said, 'I don't want to create any unpleasantness, particularly in someone else's home, but I can't remain in the same room as *that man*!' And on these words she made

178

for the door.

'Lucy,' said Sir Oscar, in that quiet voice which had been known to stop a raging prima donna in full spate, 'there are some urgent explanations to be made, and I am relying on you to help me.'

She turned and looked across the room at him, and he smiled and held out his hand to her.

'I'd rather not——' she began, but she came just the same, and, quite incredibly, he put his arm round her and said, still in that quiet voice, 'There is no reason to be afraid.'

Then he turned to Van Merton, who asked curtly, 'Whose idea was this extraordinary get-together?'

'I'm afraid it was mine,' replied Oscar Warrender, without any visible signs of regret. 'I have no wish to interfere——'

('Oh, darling!' murmured his wife on a note of humorous protest.)

'—but, as we are a family unit——' he paused for a moment to allow that extraordinary phrase to sink in—'as we are a family unit, I think we owe you some explanations and apology.'

'Shall we all sit down?' suggested Anthea, with an air of restoring normality to a very peculiar situation, and Lucy Warrender dropped into a chair, though her brother-in-law continued to stand beside her. Kate sank down on the nearby window seat and Van Merton, on sudden impulse, crossed the room and seated himself beside her.

'Well,' he said grimly to their host, 'what do you propose to tell us? That there's been a misunderstanding?

'Oh, more than one,' replied Warrender equably. 'No one is entirely blameless—which is usually the case in misunderstandings—and all should be generous enough to admit it.'

There was a tense silence, then he went on, speaking almost lightly, 'Lucy is, I'm sure, prepared to admit that some years ago she was foolishly indiscreet——'

Lucy Warrender turned sharply, as though to contradict him, but there was slight pressure from the hand which rested on her shoulder, and she desisted.

'And Van will, I hope, with equal generosity, concede that he acted on that occasion with excessive haste and harshness,' finished Oscar Warrender.

Van Merton also made as though to dispute this statement, but Kate said in an imploring whisper, 'Oh, *please*——' and he checked himself and turned whatever protest he had intended to make into, 'You could be right. But, since you said that none of us was totally blameless, perhaps you would like to tell us where *you* went wrong?'

'Certainly.' Warrender smiled slightly. 'I failed to assess the situation correctly because I was unwilling to involve myself in something I mistakenly thought unimportant. Consequently, I omitted to make clear to you that I had encouraged Kate to think seriously of the Ertlinger tour and had myself suggested you as the accompanist. The mistake was mine. I apologise.'

'You don't need to,' Kate exclaimed. '*I* was more to blame for not speaking out. I think perhaps that's how it has been all along. But I was always afraid.'

'Of what?' Van asked bluntly.

'Of your anger,' she said, and he looked extremely startled. 'I never wanted to quarrel with you. I would so much rather have been friends. But with all that unfortunate business in the family background——' she stopped and made a helpless little movement of her hands.

And at that Lucy Warrender glanced back over her shoulder at her brother-in-law, who gave her the slightest nod, the gesture he characteristically used when a nervous singer was in danger of missing her cue. She bit her lip but, as though under some compulsion, she got up from her chair and crossed the room to where Van Merton and her daughter were sitting.

'I'm sorry,' she said, clasping her hands together as though to give herself courage, and she looked straight at Van. 'It probably *was* my fault that it all started. I've avoided thinking so for years and Denis—my husband—never let me feel guilty because he was like that. But he was a just man and must have known I was in the wrong, and he would want me to speak out now.'

There was a moment of total silence while Van looked at her incredulously. Then she burst out irrepressibly, 'But you were rather awful too, weren't you?'

'Yes,' he said, 'I was pretty awful too.' And he got to his feet, took her hands and unclasped them. 'It would be paltry not to try to match your generosity. I'm sorry, Lucy Warrender. And most of all

I'm sorry that the person who suffered most was someone neither you nor I would really wish to hurt.'

'Olga, you mean?—that's to say—Kate?'

He nodded. And, not for the first time in her life, Kate's mother rushed into eager and ill-judged speech.

'I'm so *glad* you realise what a dear, good girl she is. I would hate anyone to think less of her because I was silly—(That's true, Kate dear!) And now everything is going to be all right and you can go on that concert tour after all, with Mr Merton the accompanist as you wanted. How fortunate that dear Carlo happens to be late. All the explanations have been made now before he came. But he's due any minute, isn't he?'

She was really speaking to herself, but if she had shouted the words in Van's face they could not have had a more catastrophic effect.

'Ertlinger—*here*?' He flushed dark red with obvious fury as he turned on Warrender. 'What sort of set-up is this? How much more have you been meddling in my affairs?'

'In Kate's affairs,' Sir Oscar corrected coldly. 'I'm fairly indifferent to your affairs—although you don't seem particularly good at managing them. Lucy has her timing wrong. It is tomorrow that Ertlinger is due to come and see me. I shall then, on behalf of my niece, tell him what she has finally decided about this concert tour.'

'Oh, Uncle Oscar!' Kate laughed although the tears stood in her eyes. 'How dear—and clever you are!' Then she went to him and said shyly,

'May I kiss you?'

'You may,' he said, and he took her face lightly between his hands and kissed her. 'Now it is for you to make your own decisions. I withdraw from all involvement in the present situation—which will I am sure please Anthea, who thinks I have meddled too much already.'

'I haven't said so, darling,' said Anthea. 'But it seems to me that this is the right moment for all the supporting cast to leave the stage. What about some tea, Lucy? I for one could do with some, couldn't you?—and Oscar?'

Her husband exchanged a smile with her and followed her, but Lucy hung back for a moment, looking rather as though she wanted to engage her daughter in conversation. Then Warrender turned at the door and once more held out his hand to her.

'You and I have quite a lot to talk about, Lucy,' he said pleasantly. 'You are the only person in the world who can answer the questions I should like to ask about my brother.'

And, restored to the position of someone who still had a unique function to fulfil, she smiled and went with him.

As the door closed behind them there was silence in the room. Then Van, looking intently at his shoes, said, 'Wily old fox, Warrender, isn't he?'

'He's the most wonderful man in the world,' Kate retorted indignantly.

'Oh, Kate——' he looked up and smiled ruefully across at her—'is he?'

'Well, the *second* most wonderful,' she amended, and suddenly ran to him.

He caught her in his arms and held her very close. Then he tipped up her face and kissed her several times and said almost dreamily, 'You don't know how often I've longed to do that.'

'Why didn't you do it, then?' she asked quite naturally. 'It would have saved a lot of heartache.'

'But I thought you were dazzled by Ertlinger, and more than half in love with him. Not to mention that you proposed to link your career with his.'

'I *was* a bit dazzled at first,' she conceded truthfully. 'But I was never even a quarter in love with him. Whereas——'

'Yes?' he prompted eagerly as she paused. 'Are you going to say you were about a quarter in love with me?'

'No.' Then, as he looked really anxious she capitulated entirely. 'Not a quarter or a half—but wholly.'

'Oh, Kate!' He kissed her again. 'Couldn't you have given me just the smallest hint? All those times we were working together——'

'But I didn't know then.'

'You didn't *know*? When did you find out, for heaven's sake?'

'Well——' she looked slightly ashamed—'not until you stormed out of here in a fury because it was suggested I should tour with Carlo.'

'But that's only a few days ago!'

She nodded.

'And you have the effrontery to wonder why I was jealous and bad-tempered and totally confused about your feelings?'

'I'm sorry.' She rubbed her cheek against his shoulder. 'It was rather idiotic of me. But these things just come on one suddenly, don't they? I bet you don't remember just when you first thought you loved me.'

'I most certainly do! It was that time you looked me in the eye and asked if I'd found that missing photograph, and all the time you knew—and I knew—that you'd pinched it.'

'I don't think that's a very lovable thing to remember,' she protested.

'It's kind of cute, though.' He smiled in a way Oscar Warrender would have described as fatuous, but which Kate found extraordinarily endearing. 'It was rather like a lamb putting out its tongue at the butcher.'

She laughed a good deal at this odd compliment, but looked not at all displeased. Then he frowned and became very serious as he said, 'About this concert tour—do you desperately want to team up with Ertlinger?'

'*Now?* No, of course not. Whatever gave you that idea?'

'I wouldn't want you to feel you were done out of the chance of a lifetime, just because I'd been unreasonable. I would even be willing to do the accompanying—provided you married me first.'

'No, you wouldn't,' she assured him. 'You'd be glowering every time he kissed me.'

'*Kissed* you?' He flushed angrily at the very idea.

'Of course. That's the way the Carlos of this world react. He'd say, "You were wonderful tonight, darling." Then he'd kiss me quite casually, and you'd probably knock him down before we'd got off the platform.'

'Yes, I probably would,' he agreed soberly.

'So it wouldn't do. Even if I wanted it—which I don't. What I want is to make what Sir Oscar calls "a modest career" on the concert platform, with you as my accompanist. Just the two of us together—if that doesn't fall far short of your own ambitions, that is.'

'My dear,' he said seriously, 'if you and I can work together making music, that would be the very height of my ambitions.'

'Mine too,' she agreed, and she put her hand into his as though making a pact.

It was at least twenty minutes before they stopped discussing future plans and went to join the others. No one seemed particularly surprised at the outcome of their discussion. Anthea expressed open satisfaction, Warrender observed that a certain degree of interference seemed to have been justified, and Lucy murmured, 'Well, I suppose it's all for the best.'

'I shall try to keep you of that opinion,' Van told her. Then he kissed her, at which she looked startled and then pleased. But what set the seal on a precarious new friendship was the fact that he indignantly repudiated her suggestion of a separate taxi when they were departing.

'What sort of a family arrangement is that?' he wanted to know. 'You come with us, of course.' And, with one arm round Kate and the other round Lucy, he escorted them to the lift.

Anthea came to see them off, and stood there smiling until the descending lift bore them out of sight. Then she went back thoughtfully into the flat, where she found her husband comfortably slumped in an armchair, absorbed in the score of a Mahler symphony which he was to conduct in a few days' time.

He took no notice of her and, faintly piqued, she came and leant her arms on the back of his chair and said, 'Has anyone ever told you, Oscar Warrender, that you're really a sentimentalist at heart?'

'Not in so many words.' He made a pencil note on the side of his page. 'But the thought has occurred to me once or twice during the last few days.'

Then, reaching up, he drew her hand down over his shoulder, kissed the inside of her wrist and said, 'Would you like to know my brother's opinion of you?'

'Your brother?—but he never met me.'

'He didn't need to. He drew his conclusions, so Kate tells me, from a letter of mine written after we'd been married less than a year.'

'And what did he conclude?' She smiled in an intrigued way and came round to sit on the arm of his chair.

'He said that if I hadn't married you I would have been a harder man and a lesser artist.'

'It isn't true!' exclaimed Anthea indignantly.

'Isn't it?' He laughed and put his arm round her. 'Well, which of us can say? But he added something else, my clever brother. He said that the greatest piece of good fortune ever to come my way was to marry you. And on that I will have no argument—even from you,' said Oscar Warrender as he pulled her down against him and kissed her.

Harlequin® Plus

A WORD ABOUT THE AUTHOR

Readers of Mary Burchell's novels have long ago gathered that she is an opera fan. What they may not know is that her whole writing career stems from the fact that she and her sister, Louise, shared a passionate interest in opera and its stars.

Mary Burchell was brought up to believe that if she wanted something very much she had to go out and get it for herself. And as a young woman, what she and Louise wanted more than anything else was to hear the great opera star Galli-Curci perform in New York City. So they set to work saving, and two years later were on their way to America to hear their idol.

As a result of this adventure, Mary wrote her first article—for a small fashion newspaper. And on the strength of this article she was offered her first writing job. Gradually she discovered that she had a flair for writing romantic fiction, and to date she has written more than seventy-five Romances and Presents, many with exciting operatic backgrounds.

Legacy of
PASSION
BY CATHERINE KAY

A love story begun long ago comes full circle…

Venice, 1819: Contessa Allegra di Rienzi, young, innocent, unhappily married. She gave her love to Lord Byron—scandalous, irresistible English poet. Their brief, tempestuous affair left her with a shattered heart, a few poignant mementos—and a daughter he never knew about.

Boston, today: Allegra Brent, modern, independent, restless. She learned the secret of her great-great-great-grandmother and journeyed to Venice to find the di Rienzi heirs. There she met the handsome, cynical, blood-stirring Conte Renaldo di Rienzi, and like her ancestor before her, recklessly, hopelessly lost her heart.
